PIG

Kitty Fitzgerald was born in Ireland and raised in Yorkshire. She has written drama for the BBC, for the theatre and for film, as well as fiction and poetry. *Pigtopia* has been published in eighteen territories to date, and was awarded second place in the 2005 Barnes and Noble Discover Award for Fiction. She lives in Northumberland.

Further praise for *Pigtopia*:

'Stunningly moving . . . a tour de force, confronting us with the daily meanness of life yet celebrating the small flickers of kindness that ease the suffering.' *Los Angeles Times*

'Redemption through sacrifice marks Pigtopia . . . and in the end, as all good stories do, it takes us places both familiar and fantastic.' *Washington Post*

'A heartbreaking story of intolerance, friendship and sacrifice, told in evocative prose and with great love.' *Richmond Times*

'Through the relationship of Jack and Holly, the novel suggests the importance of remaining open to the everyday wonders of the world and of realizing the holiness of life within the ordinary.' *Times Literary Supplement*

'A grim fairytale, but one told with passion and sympathy. The voices of Jack and Holly, alternate narrators, are ingeniously realised.' *Daily Mail*

'The great delicacy with which Fitzgerald renders that relationship raises Pigtopia well above the norm in contemporary fiction.' *Montreal Gazette*

'[Pigtopia] hovers between the strange and wonderful.' *New York Times*

'Satisfying and heart breaking . . . This beautifully crafted story retells the classic lesson of Mary Shelley's Frankenstein.' *Publishers Weekly*

'Enchanting and tragic . . . there's no denying this novel's sweet-tempered blend of wonder, heartbreak and, of course, "pigsense".' *Salon*

'Pigtopia is a spell-binding story, part Greek myth and part Charlotte's Web. Kitty Fitzgerald weaves pig-husbandry and pastoral poetry into a beautiful lament.' Lyall Watson, author of *The Whole Hog*

'Fascinating. A strange and moving book.' David Almond, author of *Skellig*

KITTY FITZGERALD

Pigtopia

faber and faber

First published in 2005
by Faber and Faber Limited
3 Queen Square London WC1N 3AU
This paperback edition first published in 2006

Typeset in Sabon by Faber and Faber Ltd
Printed in England by Mackays of Chatham plc,
Chatham, Kent

A CIP record for this book
is available from the British Library

ISBN 978–0–571–22732–7
ISBN 0–571–22732–5

2 4 6 8 10 9 7 5 3 1

For Caitlin and Peter

ONE

Dad was a porker

Mam says that dad was pigflesh and pigmind, a huge mucky porker what nabbed her by force, then jogtrotted off beyond the farlands when he understood what had been hatched. She cursed a thick sable stripe what grew, she says, full stretch of his bony back and pearly underfur, layered below bristling skin what she named brutesigns. But I am in memory of a tickly jacket beside my hogface, unclammy energetic hands with blondie hairs creeping up on wrists, and loud laughs what went far high and lowdown like music. The only porky thing of dad was the sucking snore he gave fell asleep sideways on the sofa. I am in memory of him until I was twelve birth days gone, after that he was not. Mam says my head is bulky as a hog's on account of dad was pig. She says my brain is mush, like pig slops, on that purpose.

'He was a no-good swine, a pig of the highest order,' she shouts, when whisky has her.

Times when I had less years on me she would step me,

unclothed, up on chairs to scout for sable and pearl fur and she would scrub at my hide for undergrowth. There was blood pressed out with these scrubs and I dropped stealthy tears within pillows and jumpers so as not to stir her more. Hogboy's voice was not a welcome thing any much time, but less once pigdad was no more.

I believe there is prospects in mam's words of my pigness because my head is fat and squashed, with a snout, and heavy as a pig's must be, with eyes as gobbets of coal. Though there isn't trotters or a curlicue tail, I some times splat down to run free with piggywigs what I love, as they is brothers and sisters in my tribe, and because they love me full on. And one long time back I made dreams of my very own furbristle tail what swished and throbbed as the hearts of birds in humanpig hands.

Pigs and me have understanding of our lacking of limits, eyes lock up on certain sounds or the twirl of air with movements. A sharply dab of rear trotter tells pigs is uneasy, a quick paddling by front hooves makes sign of pleasure. Snorts and snufflings have especial own meanings. How much, highlow pitch, deepness and tang, all speak differing things. I hear of sadness within my tunnel ears, I share their joy fullness and they hand up big love.

Jack Plum is my given name. Sharp and sweet, dad said, as the freshly plucked apple. I am the ten-to-one mam can not walk. I am the blame of her wobbly legs and such constant pain what nags at her back like rats' teeth crunching at bone. I came out of her most wrong, arse first, elbows angled up, fists stuck at the forehead, ripping flesh, wrenching innards with my big broad head, snaffling at her breasts like the hungry litter. I never cried as baby, mam says, only screeched and grunted and snuffled, and trotted on all fours from three months of ageing.

Someplace, way within this massive head space, I still catch echoes of dadsongs about long gone times when pigs did fly. The songs have words of giants what walked up on Earth and suffering little children being saved by a tidal wave. His songvoice was deep, deep as the old well in Farmer Cotton's far field, on the cusp of the farlands, and tart like lemonbuns grandma used to churn up before she got to live with Jee Sus. There lurks a small slice of dad-voice within the hog skull what rocks me into sleep many nights when rest is extreme hard to get, or the troublesome hogbrain can not find comfort any where.

The lemonbun grandma was of dad's stock and was not to be welcomed in our homespace, so mam said often when her spitting tongue was out and about.

'She's a wild pig too, a mad sow,' mam would shout in the warpath voice, if dad said grandma lemonbun should come to visiting. And his face would fall down to gloomy folds and he would bite at his lips till blood leaked off and I would watch and give wishes for loving to find some path to come up between them.

When dad was awayoff with his butchering job, mam

whispered the nasties into my hogboy ears. She liked to spread hatewords like dad spread butter on morningtoast, thick and melting in. I would close my inside ears off and think into a differing space where her voice was blunt like rain on high shed roofs. Some times, in this space, I got to see bright lit flames sparking from out her head.

Dad had give me tellings about mam's sourness in a young age. He told of sickness what blanketed her since my hatching and how she would not have doctors what she hated. Deep pression he named it but impressed up on me not to take hurt or bother from her malignancy on account the troublesome stuff was not of my making. That was the broad time what I took notice how people's talk does slip out in differing ways. If it spurts the side ways it is mostly cross or full with spite or misery, but if it flows frontwise it is mostly true and honey.

Often, when dad made the return from his butcher days, mam would screech the 'reek of death' was on him and name him 'walking bloodbath' and tell him to go from her. That is when he and me would take our selves below, to cellar ground, to prank with my trains. Dad had made up a showering box there and a cupboard for fresh clothes to linger in. These times he would make his radio songvoice, along with the scrub a dub, and I did manage tracks and stations for some trains all by my own. Sometimes the slithersounds would come down at us, from voices within mam's TV, dropped between flooring boards, and just some moments, we got to hear mam's laugh. Then me and dad would splat hands because a small goodness had turned up to brighten life.

Before dad was gone he unfurled plans for our yet-to-come-time and made work on the digging out of a palace for pigs, from the starting of the cellar, out beyond fields by Pardes Wood. It was to become a 'large adventure' and he said we would make the creation of it side up on side. I helped splodge a wall down and we burrowed into sooty earth like minermen or moles sniffing at air. And all as full secret, nappying hammers and picks with ragged towels and doing especial work if mam was gone out or in the whisky sleep. It was dad's daytime dream to breed his own piggies, not chop them to chumps at Blandish butchers with his sharp, shiny tools. He told he'd had plenty of chopping flesh and bone for people's pots and pans. His desire was to make growing things, see runty piglets nurtured into grand sows and hogs from his efforting.

For all of the hard working time we did, dad made his songvoice or told me fresh things on life. I came to know the way he had been nurtured up on a farm place in a valley named Eden, which dad called a paradise place. I have memory of all this kept safe.

'I was the youngest of four brothers, Jack,' he told, 'and so the land would have been a long time coming into my hands, that's why I studied butchery.'

I understood, from his mouth shape, that he was regret

full of this. When I have the fears and frights in the bottomless dark time I think on that valley called Eden and wonder at those brothers and that land. And I make a dream that some time I will go to that place to find dad in happiness there and welcoming of me.

One midnight time, beyond the digging of our hands into soreness all long day, dad fetched me into Farmer Cotton's piglands and gathered a large sow up for riding. He had told of pigriding in a past time and recognised that I wanted to know it and be it. The bristling body next my short trousered legs was not fear full to me, it was suet pud warm and the furbristle tail, it was just as the one of my dreamtime. Dad showed the ear touch for the steering and the kittensoft pressing with knees to stop or turn. He threaded up a cat bell on soft purply ribbon for the sow's neck and all the while, as me and pig larked along, dad ran aside us making sweet songs which all the pigs liked, and this cat bell, it trilled and chirped till my lop ears hummed full with delight.

Dad left his own butchering tools at his going, swaddled within oiled cloth, whiffing of blood and spit and hidden alleys swilling of red water and gore stuff. I maintain them clean and sharp, for his return, but tucked up far from pigs so they can not fear 'the end'. Creatures what live among humanpigkind have come to absorb our killing signs.

After dad did not come back for some many days and mam screamed that he had 'abandoned us without a back ward glance', I made the choice to do the completing of dad's pig venture. It was not a task of simpleness but I finished the Pig Palace all by my own work. Week up on week up on month up on year, digging and shaping and sweating with the strength of soil and stones. I would linger often times next the skeletons of little creatures, trapped in and out of mud layers, to try and know their full picture, like what they once was and the manner of the dying. And I would be out long times beyond darkfall seeking for buildwork at houses and I would gather cement and bricks and wood and other things I had no names to give but had seen dad's use of. I fashioned up this cart, like the pony does have, for my hog hands to drag about full of thrown out or borrowed stuff. Some of my build up items are not too proper, not good edges and shapes, but I struggled to uncover ways of making and I kept on dad's plan what he had drawn in the school book.

These were the darktimes where I came to know the big metal boxes where people throwed things and I learned that name from listening, it is 'skip'. These were times when I made discovery of dustbin days, of things being put out what could be of much usefulness to me. I was like a whiskerful tomcat, prowling and purring through darktime streets and I did get treasure for the Pig Palace. Such things as, pretend grass, pretend flowers, shiny colour full paper and hangdown balls for decoration, metal buckets and manysize bowls.

Mam still does not know of the Pig Palace. She expects I play with trains still, way down in the cellar where her wheelchair will not roll, and I go along with that. It is my own especial place, with water from Pardes Wood stream, what ripples deep in the old water hose, and grass and pretend flowers from the dustbin days and cat bells what dad fetched to rig out forthcoming pigs so they would not get astray on their nightly outside romping within woods and water.

My firstly pigs, at year one, were secret borrowed from Farmer Cotton's early litterings and I did return them with the extra sow in year two. There was some early failings what died and got put within Farmer Cotton's pens for his disposing methods. And I made up some special goodbye singing with my left pig tribe on the losing of them. Farmer Cotton has the chunky motoring lorry with slatty wood sidings for transports of animals live and dead. I do not know what he fathomed of his changing pigwig residents but now I am many years and many litters gone, and today Freya, my bestest sow, brings more. She has fashioned the piggylets delivering nest and pants and mewls so Nodger, the dad of the piggylets to come, snorts close, nudging at her with the snout and dropping fresh grass at her mouth to make comfort with taste and moisture.

I know of all this pigbirthing stuff from dad's many tellings. It is from the wild time of pigs that sows make groupings with their daughterpigs and other sows. Humanpigs have named this 'sounders' but I like to say 'tribes' as it is a gathering word. Many litter generations share the territory space and join in with the piggylet rearing stuff. An other thing dad told was about newborn piggylets, how they slurp one especial teat on their mamsow and use it all times.

Freya's time is now full come. I see the makings of a piggylet slurping. That is one! Freya squeals the pain and joy fullness of it and Nodger comes lost in the squirmy shape of his first youngling, licking and rolling it at Freya's teats until Nancy sow trolls him away from the tribe area. Here is the next come slumpering out, good Freya. She knows how it must go.

Way up above us, within the housespace, mam smoulders with in the wheelchair, lonely and angry, always angry. She hammers at the floor with her big stick, banging for me to attend by her. I pretend I am not hearing until Freya has squelched up six piggywigs. But mam begins the bellows as well as the banging and her sideways voice rips at me with all its misery so that I must go to her.

'Must leave now,' I tell to Freya, because piggywigs need to know of my comings and goings, need to know my return will arrive. 'Big sorry, back later. Yes. And now . . . quiet . . . must be as snow blanket, as leaf falling, as feathers dancing.' I get the grumpsnort by Freya and Nodger snouts me to the upsteps.

Mam has expectation of noise from the cellar when I am

below but not other points of time, so these pigs have learned about the softening when I am gone. Clever, kind pigs. And there is mam, all worked up into meanness and blaming me.

'Useless creature,' she says at sight of me, 'never there when you're wanted, always hanging around when you're not.'

Mam's eyes have the whiskysoup look of extra meanness, not the companion glance of the pigs, who want closeness. She will put hurt up on me if I am not wary, it is her way. She has been entirely insidedoors since many years gone and refuses exit at all times. No freshness of air enfolds her, ever, and I cannot enjoy the stink of her. When she has the drunksleeps I bash open all windows and let juicy wind in, to bring scents of grass and flowers and whispered words from farlands and near.

One time or other I do see within the despair she keeps holded in and I do know all the blame is on me, and those instants my tongue does grow and try to choke breath away for ever. It is like a dread thing, dad did say. This voice of mine did never work its right way in the space surround mam, I do hold no memory of it inside the hogskull. I do still make the attempt of words to soften her misery.

'Y . . . you . . . b . . . been . . . drink . . . ing . . . wh . . . wh . . . whisky,' I say.

As is usual my words is all halted up and broken apart when they are out loud in mam's space or in the outside world. This boarmouth will not work proper and the throat parches up like sandy storms. Withinside the huge head, talk does make real sound, perhaps eloquent, but it gushes into the open all garbled up and wrong.

Mam laughs and turns the air cold. 'I want my tea! Look at the clock! It's way past time for my tea. I think you do it on purpose. Eh? You do, don't you?'

She skewers at me with her fat stick but I am too speedy. I learned, way past times, to dodge fists and weapons. I start the makings of her tea and do not make arguing because she will not listen to much of my sounds. Why would she, in the age it takes for words to shape themselves? By the clock I'm only two minutes of lateness but she enjoys the stickbangs. Blam, bang, blam. The linofloor is dented and pocked up but she does not care. No body ever comes within the house space. They are fear full at Jack Plum, overgrown goblin, or they have some jaggedness of mam's peeved tongue. Mam's deep misery stuff pushed all sometime visitors far off and away long time back.

We is placed at the very edge slice of the house rows what nudge the beginnings of Pardes Wood and that is of excellence for pigs and me. It keeps us part away from other house sounds and is not a passing place without you want entrance to the wood.

'And don't turn those daft, dribbly eyes on me,' mam goes on. 'You're the reason I can't walk. You! With your big empty head stuck inside me. Don't you ever forget what you did to me!'

I would not forget ever as she reminders me all days.

When she is not TV goggling mam plays favourite music up on the player of tapes. Mostly Donovanman as he makes the sad lonely habit she seeks. She wallows, like pigs in water, that is something dad telled.

'Stop wallowing,' he said, oftentimes, and, 'stop feeling sorry for yourself.' Always, as he mouthed things I spoke his words inside my hogskull to make the lips take proper shape and to twist breath for the forming of them. This was the way I held on to many words inside and said them loud at alone times. Within hoghead there is vastness of memory space which I hold on to strongly.

Mam had her everytime words to hurl back at dad when he said the wallowing stuff, it was an expected return, like a boy at church altar I saw one longtime back. The priestly man did say his especial words and the boy at altar did respond his own and this did go on long times. Dad did say this way, mam did speak that way, extreme regular. Her tongue spurted these words as gunbullets, rat, brat, trat. Stuff on how he abandoned and stopped loving and made a monster, which is me. Times happened when dad rushed on to his knees, close by to her, and gave pleads for mam to see doctors and get helped and to get up off the wheelchair. And all of it lost on her, all his words squashed to nothing next her big wretchedness.

I consider she has no remembrance ever of happytimes or of contentment, or if she does, it is maybe like the shadow what lands on her face oftentimes but melts quick as snow on fire. She sings with her music until the hiccy coughs come and I rush tea in before she begins more bellowing stuff. I lay up the tray nice, with the flowery cloth, milk in that jug with hollyhocks around and sugar in the goldrim bowl.

'Th . . . there y . . . you are . . . m . . . mm . . . mam . . . my,' I say, my voice constantly in refusal to be whole.

'Don't call me that!' she says. 'And put the mug here, not there!'

She turns her back from me then, for the whiskypour within her tea. When she looks to me again she wears her crafty, spite full eyes. 'I wanted to get rid of you,' she says, 'I wanted to flush you down the pan, but your swine of a dad wouldn't hear of it. He persuaded me to keep you, and where is he now, eh? Where's your pig of a dad? I believed in him, Jack. I dreamed everything would be okay, that we would be happy families, until I saw you dribbling and drooling out of that boar's head.'

I heard of this telling oftentimes, more times than a miser stacks his money, was dad's words. I do not think she has intention of hurting, she just can not stop the meanness coming into her because it *is* all of my fault, the trap with the wheelchair, dad gone, all of that. She sits day up on day to think around nothing much else. There is no want to be outside on her ownsome and there is no allowing of me to push her on account of the ugliness. People laugh or gaze or run from me and as the hogmouth can not speak words in proper form, mam has no belief in my under standing.

Without the pigs I would be forsaken of love and perhaps I could turn into anger shapes like mam does and want to put out blame. I know these types of stirrings, the want to make hurt, and I believe I could lash great damages and stomp stuff to dust if it took me. Some times, mostly in the dark moments or on the edge of dreamthoughts or in memory spaces, I have the longing of an other to make words with. A humanpig who does not mess my mouth up with the blaming, one who listens to my insidethoughts and speaks out theirs. I have had the inmost thoughts on this extra many times and I have done the watching, beyond windows, out at the road, in the light and at dark times into opencurtained spaces. I gathered with my lop ears, I snouted the smell of strange humanpigs, stared into the shape of them, insideout, and at their space between others. In all of this seeking time there is one, one best humanpiggirl what is named Holly Lock.

I watch her without on the road, herding with the other kiddypigs, stomping round, screeching louder than tribes of boars, and Holly Lock, with them but not with them. Some thing always held back, not shared, not used up, hid within her. She goes mulching to Pardes Wood on her ownsome, picking and poking amongst the moss full plantings, taking up leaves, singing, reading of books, listening at music and sometimes plodging within the stream. Holly Lock, named as a tree. Her mam calls the word in two pieces, Hol . . . ly! I make the shape of it inside my hogskull and it does come out right, Holly, Holly Lock.

Following from what dad did on the pig thing, I did draw my own venture plans some times back. It is to make an attachment with Holly for the aloneplace in us both to become a connecting thing. I dream of it, waketime and sleeptime, Jack Plum and Holly Lock putting words together and making laughs. There is always much laughs within the dreamtime. And I plan that we do troll on the pigpaths within the wood and I explain to her of the inmost boarpaths what dad telled using ancient naming, like Torc. Pigs full of sacred and divineness. And at my pigs' outside nighttime plodge place is way old carvings on rock, of relic symbols what I will show to her. Dad did find these one long time back and that was the decision for pig plodging place made. They is of true rareness, dad telled, and has to be guarded from destructions. They does come about in wild boar time when the god dess what dad named De Meter did dance together with pigs of great sacredness and they did stay within in her temples. I made a name for this rock carving what is pigrelicstone.

It is round as pigs' bellies with marks of the boar head and an ear ring of spirals and on the sides is markings of double lines and comb and mirrors what dad telled is most especial for pig divine stuff. I make blessings there on many moontimes for this plan of connection with Holly Lock and she will see this one time soon.

I have big memory stuff to share with her as one time when dad took me to those Hoppings at the Townmoor and bought pinkish candyfloss which got stuck all in my hair and teeth. He took no bother from the staring at me or the turned away sharp murmurings, he looked full in their eyes, like a dare for them, to name me, monster. Some did, but from longish distances and dad would look to me and say, 'They're cowards, Jack, and we don't have time to spare for cowards. Life's too short for that.' And those times he telled too of these mysterypigs waygone, of names like Orc Traith, huge boars of taletelling but filled with the magic. All of these I will tell on to Holly for her own memory keeping.

Holly Lock has never done the laughs at me or slinged stones or grass sods as some of the other spiky kiddypigs does. Some is as angry as mam, boiling away inside, as volcanoes wanting to erupt and burn destruction on adults and sometimes animals. They must not know of my Pig Palace; never hear the song full way a sow does croon her newborns into slumber; never know the cleverness of porkers, or the way their flesh and our flesh can knit together, as brothers and sisters below skin.

Some years past Holly Lock had a huge birth day time partying and all kiddypigs danced in the road and punched balloons up and about. Her mam placed a big bright thing up and it did flutter words: *Happy Birthday Holly, Eleven Years Old Today.* I asked mam of the words and then I made the mark on my calendar, that one Blandish the butcher still delivers us on Christmas time, with drawings of how pigs and cows are made of chops and liver and bacon. I listened and waited and watched and kept it in memory time year up on year up on year until my front brain space told it was time to make the approach. I look within now and I see the place and check the mark on the calendar. It is the coming time of an other Holly birth day. Part of my planning was this waiting, this giving of offerings and making right the time of connection. Now is it, this birth date of four teen years and the pigrock blessing is strong. I must make a gift just as is destined and I will try for the alliance of me and the pigs and Holly Lock.

From the upsteps inside window I make notice when Holly Lock leaves the pack of shrieking kiddypigs and strolls her way beyond, on to the lane what leads only to Pardes Wood. None follows her on. They do not relish woods, except the hunting ones of guns and noise and I do scent when they is approaching long way off. The tall girlpig with the dropdown mouth what is named Samantha makes notice she is gone, but flings back into the trick of jumping with the board of rollers, up slopeys and down, leaps and slides. I cut along at the edge of my garden and follow, making out of sight as Holly strides the stream to stare at the mumbling water and pokes at under growth as if she is searching for treasure. This is the time, the years-long waiting time and there is the struggle of my mouth to make words straight when my breath is not good at all.

'H . . . HH . . . Ho . . . Holl . . . olly . . . LLL . . . o . . . ock,' is how it comes.

She stands tall up as startled sheep to face at me, offside and near snorting. She puts me in mind of Freya pig, but I make no laugh in case I put the frighteners on her.

'Go away, Jack Plum,' she says, 'I'm not allowed to talk to you.'

I watch her eyes close now, closer than I has ever been. They is bright copper brown and extra big as they stare out to me.

'HH . . . HH . . . Hap . . . py . . . BB . . . B . . . BBBir . . . thd . . . ay . . . HHH . . . HHolly,' I say.

'It's not my birthday till tomorrow,' she says, and her eyes dart beyond to see signs of any humanpig up on the path. There is not one, my lop ears tell me that. I manage to make the words of a gift at her and shuffle one step near. She paces back and almost stumbles up on the glossy shale and wet grass. I move for to help but she does not like that.

'Keep away from me or I'll scream!' she makes the warning.

I keep extra still and make the promise of no hurt. I say about ugly being not always cruelty. She does not like my words and makes an other glance for the path beyond. It is not happening as the plan in my dream went and I have confusion. I have need to know why she is so feared and is it just my big hoghead and ugliness? I can not get the words without my mouth, except *why?*

'Because,' she says.

'Why?' I make again, as a lowdown sound not screamy and it is out of puzzlement.

'Leave me alone,' she says. 'Go on, clear off.'

She runs at me with girlpig hands bunched as tight fists, and she would punch and kick through if she had need. I move far so she can run the path towards the road. As she sprints she shouts the mam word and I know it was not the time of fulfilling. Tomorrow is the birth day, she said, and that is a right time to make a connect and take her to Pig Palace. And this nighttime, trolling at the magic pigrelic-stone, I will give extra tributes of dandelion and beechnut before the return of Nodger to Farmer Cotton's pods.

TWO

Holly Lock's world

Y'know when you wake up from a frightening dream, how the edges of everything are blurred, like the everyday picture of the world hasn't had time to come back. Well, when I was there, standing so close to Jack Plum, it was like things had shifted just a little bit, like it wasn't real time. All the way up the uneven path from the wood I felt as if I was wading in custard. I didn't look behind at all, just kept going and I had a stitch by the time I got to the others.

It had all dropped back into place by then, no more fuzziness. Samantha's bored face was sharp and clear. She lives on our street and she calls herself my best friend but she's always going off and trying out new girls or getting a boyfriend, then I don't see her outside school for weeks and weeks, till it all goes wrong, which it always does. She can get a bit clingy and people don't like that, sometimes it freaks me. Because she's very pretty she gets away with a lot. Anyway, she was fed up of the skateboarding competition and wanted me to join a team for a game of cricket but I shrugged her off. She'd just come back to me after getting really close to this girl Paula for a few weeks, so I didn't see why I should do everything she wanted all of a sudden. I thought she was going to complain, as per usual when I said I was going home, but she didn't, something just shifted behind her eyes like she was notching up my faults. Or maybe I was feeling a bit paranoid. My legs were unsteady and I wanted to be in my bedroom, alone, to think about what had happened, so I didn't give a damn.

I lay on the bed for about half an hour. My head was all sort of frantic, hopping about from one thing to another and I wasn't sure if I was trembling because I was still scared or if it was just relief. It's funny about dreams, how they make this world seem unreal and how you get similar feelings when you're frightened, like it all goes out of focus for a few seconds. I mean, I was only metres away from our house when Jack Plum spoke to me but I felt as if I was in some other, unexpected place. Mam says I've got an 'excess of imagination' as if it's some sort of hormone imbalance but maybe it's all just chemicals.

I calmed down slowly and then began asking myself questions. I mean, how did Jack Plum know when my birthday was? It was a surprise to me that he knew my name as I didn't even know he could talk. Then I thought, what if he'd been stalking me, like those nutters do, following me, digging through the rubbish in our bin looking for information. But he didn't try to stop me, when I started to run, and he could have, the size of him.

When I felt better I got up and looked at myself in the long mirror. Too small, too skinny, no breasts, mad hair, doggy sort of a face, more like a lad than a lass. Why would anyone want to stalk me? I was a runt, that's what dad used to call me before he took off. He said if I'd been born a dog, I'd have been dumped at birth. Charming. Mam always took my side when he went on about me not being pretty, she reckoned she'd been a bit of a tomboy herself. But, whenever she bought clothes for me they were always a bit too big or a bit too flouncy, like she was secretly willing me to grow up.

My room is great, I chose the colours, the bedding and the blinds. Green's my favourite colour, all shades of green, but especially the darker ones, like emerald, viridian, olive. I've got an en suite shower, bath, wash basin and toilet with sage-green tiles. Next to the wide window there's a wood and metal plant stand. This is cool because I want to work with plants when I leave school. Not sure what exactly I want to do, maybe train to be a botanist. What I'd really love is to discover a new species of plant and have it named after me. That's why I go into Pardes Wood. It's a very old coniferous forest and there's always the chance of finding something unusual. I was on the hunt for a ghost orchid today, *Epipogium aphyllum*. It's only been seen above ground a couple of times in the past century and apparently likes the shady area below beech trees. There's plenty of those in Pardes Wood, especially at this end.

Saxifrage is one of my favourite plants, *Saxifraga sarmentosa*, better known as Mother of Thousands. The little plants at the end of the runners can grow as long as sixty centimetres. I've got one hanging above my bathroom window with the extensions drooping right down over the glass like old lace.

On my stand there's *Paphiopedilum callosum*, slipper orchid; *Ipheion uniflorum*, spring starflower, the Froyle Mill variety which has beautiful purple flowers; *Felicia amelloides*, kingfisher daisy; and my absolute favourite, *Pelargonium graveolens crispum*, lemon geranium. It smells fabulous all the time but when you pinch and rub the leaves between your fingers it's heavenly. It's a very thirsty little beast but it doesn't like being misted.

Mam got home while I was watering the plants, I heard her in the kitchen. I thought of telling her about Jack Plum but then remembered that I shouldn't have been in the woods alone anyway.

It was pepperoni pizza for tea, followed by strawberry cheesecake. My choice. Mam and me take it in turns to choose what we eat. It's really so she can make me eat proper food every other day but that's okay because I can choose anything I want on my days. And after tea on Fridays we always have a quiz and score points. I do one set of questions and she does another. The first to get twenty points is owed a favour, like she sometimes wants help with the ironing or I want some new music.

I like it at home. Just me and mam, it's relaxing, but I couldn't let on at school, everyone's always moaning on about their parents splitting up, not giving them enough pocket money, grounding them for no good reason, or not letting them smoke, etc. etc. I'm lucky, I guess, because when dad left things got better. No more of him griefing us all the time. Being on my own's good but I'm not that comfortable in a group, never know what to say, unlike Samantha who can rabbit on for hours. Sometimes I go through the motions, hang out, pretend I'm enjoying myself, you've got to. If I owned up at school that I'd rather stay in and watch a video with my mam than hang around the dingy precinct sharing a bottle of cider and a joint, they'd think I was crazy.

Sometimes I do wonder why dad didn't love me enough to stay and why he's never bothered to get in touch, not even at Xmas time or birthdays.

The pizzas were already in the oven when I got downstairs. I could smell the garlic. The radio was turned low on one of those 1970s hits stations and mam was wiggling about to the music, trying to sing along with it but she only knew a few of the lyrics, as usual. My mam knows the first lines of hundreds of songs and she doesn't always get them right. She was a punk when she was a teenager, I've seen photos of her with a Mohican hairdo and six earrings in each ear. Black clothes were all the rage then and she's saved some in a trunk in case the fashion comes back. Now she wears her hair long, it's dark and very glossy and she likes long skirts and bright-coloured tops, sort of ageing hippy style.

I said, 'Hi,' and she replied, 'Hello, sweetheart, everything okay?'

'Yeah, fine,' I said. She handed me the knives and forks to lay the table and just then one of her favourite songs came on the radio and she grabbed me and made me dance round the kitchen with her.

Does he love you
How can you know
How can you tell if he loves you so
Is it in his eyes . . .

When the song ended we were both out of breath. We dropped on to the kitchen chairs laughing like mad and I suddenly thought: I don't care if I never grow up. Sometimes the other girls at school talk about boys and sex in a way that scares me and I just don't feel like I'm ready for it. I'm not sure if it's because of how I feel about my body not being developed, or more than that.

Bodies are strange. What's on the outside doesn't always match up with what's on the inside. Like I feel very mature for my age but I don't look it and Jack Plum looks like a monster but his voice was sweet and soft. He also looks like an adult but doesn't act like one. Truth was, I had no idea how old he was, or what was really wrong with him. I'd always been told to keep out of his way, to leave him alone, just like all the other kids round here. Usually, he stayed away from us as well.

'Mam, y'know Jack Plum?' I said casually. 'Is he a boy or is he a man?'

'Why are you asking about Jack Plum?' she said.

'School project,' I replied, this is always the best tactic if mam's worried as school work is sacred in our house.

'A school project about Jack Plum?' she went on, as we sat down to eat. She obviously wasn't convinced.

'Yeah, Special Needs and all that, y'know.' Only a small lie.

'Oh,' she said, 'okay. Well, I'd probably say he's neither a man or a boy, he's a mixture of both.'

I tried to concentrate on eating for a while but my curiosity kept niggling at me.

'What happened to Jack Plum? Was he born like that, with that massive head or did he have an accident?'

'He was born that way.'

'Is he dangerous, mam?'

'It's difficult,' she said, after a pause.

'What is?'

'Well, nobody really knows what's wrong with Jack Plum.'

'Has he ever done anything bad?'

She looked right at me and her face was sort of sad.

'No, Holly,' she said, 'I don't think Jack Plum's ever done anything wrong.'

'So he's not dangerous then?'

'Is this really for a project?'

'Yes,' I insisted. Only way to get a straight answer.

'He's never been in trouble as far as I know and I don't think he's dangerous, Holly, but you never can tell. I've not seen much of him since he was a boy, because he hides himself away, as you know, but I just don't think you can ever be really sure with people like Jack Plum. I mean, he's been alone with his mother all this time and she's a very unpleasant woman. Okay?'

'D'you know her then, Mrs Plum?'

'No, not really. She's lived round here all her life but she's older than me and . . .'

'What about the dad? Where's he at?'

'Enough questions for now, time for my bath. We'll have the pudding later, okay?'

It was my turn to wash up so I tuned in to Radio 1 and listened to the charts. Mam came back in her dressing gown looking shiny and hot. She cheered up during the quiz because she loves cheesecake and she scored twenty points. When we watched TV, sitting together on the big sofa, she hugged me tight until it was time to do my homework. Biology and French, not too mind numbing.

It was dark when I'd finished. I stared out at the street and saw Colin Driver and his lot hanging around, trying to look cool with tabs hanging out of their mouths and baseball caps pushed up. Bloody chavers. Then I went downstairs to say goodnight and do mam's evening ritual with her.

Before Gran and Grandad Logan went to live in Canada they gave us loads of stuff and one thing mam loves is this old tarot pack. She says it was bought in China over a hundred years ago by some relative who was in the Merchant Navy. The pictures are really beautiful but you have to be careful because they're hand painted. Anyway, every night mam lays the twenty-two cards of the Major Arcana out, face down, and picks one card. This is supposed to give her guidance on how best to act the following day. She likes me to be with her when she does it because Gran Logan said I had 'good energy', whatever that means. It all seems a bit haphazard to me but I wouldn't say that to mam.

She got the 'Death' card. It always makes me shiver, even though mam says it's got nothing to do with death and everything to do with change. There's this skeleton dressed in armour riding a white horse and holding a black flag with a rose and the roman numerals for thirteen on it. In front of him is a holy man and two females, one very young. In the background the sun is coming up behind a strange landscape with a tower on the horizon.

'It represents a positive change, Holly,' she tells me.

'Changing old ways of thinking. Thirteen was a lucky number in days gone by.' If you say so, mam.

Back in my room Jack Plum kept drifting into my head. He'd always been there, in that scruffy house at the entrance to Pardes Wood, hiding himself away. We were all terrified of passing his house when we were little. Now, Colin taunts him sometimes, if his mates are around, but he's still scared underneath. You can tell by his eyes and the way he always looks ready to run. It was definitely weird, Jack Plum trying to talk to me like that, wishing me happy birthday, like there was some purpose to it, almost like he knew me.

In bed, I was restless, kept getting knotted up in the duvet then getting cold when I threw it off. I got up while it was still dark to fetch some juice from the kitchen. My mouth felt sour and dry. Before I got back into bed I turned the lights off to peep out into the street. It was dark and gloomy in between the patches of light from the lampposts and I could almost imagine someone lurking in the shadows, watching. Then I saw Jack Plum, striding along the road pulling a cart piled up high with bits of wood. He looked up at my window as he passed and raised his hand in a wave. As I dropped the curtain my body flashed with heat. For a few seconds I couldn't tell if I was awake or dreaming.

THREE

Pig Palace

Mr postalman fetches much cards to Holly Lock's house on this day of her birth and even a box within bright sparkly paper. Up on the step of her house she takes in all the stuff with two hands and big smiles. It is the Saturday, kiddypigs is all off from the school, soon they will throng about seeking for adventures, or troubles, whatever comes first.

Last dark time, when I transported piggywigs into the outsideworld for exercise and snaffle, the moon came blue, and showed water droplets on their haunches like forget-me-nots and sapphires. I turned this hogface at the skies, placed these hands on pigrelicstone, found Boar star and said wishes for Holly Lock to connect at me. I have belief that some wishtimes do bring happenings, not all, since them for dad's comeback have not been enforced. And later dark time when I trolled the trap about for woodstuff, I saw Holly in her window and that was some signal of magic working at me.

Down in Pardes Wood edges now, wind blows tunes

through high leaves in trees, the big train gushes by in distance, it goes places I will not see ever or know. Holly Lock balances her big milky pumps on stepstones what bridge the stream. She is full white girlpig this day, all but for dark dots in the shirt. She takes me in memory of the Baldinger Spotted piggy what breeds in an other land named Ger Many. I see it in the rearing pig book what dad got and he said its name and stuff about it. Like they named it 'tiger-marked' and also that it is no more, extinct, dad said. But one was found, it can and was, long time past, breed-crossed with Berkshire pigs in this land.

I watch Holly at still distance and smell up this wispy day that has just shreds of wind. There is burning pigflesh leaking into here from some houses and I make inside wishes for it to veer far from Pig Palace. It is not settling for pigsnouts. As well as pigflesh is toast scent, some with charred on it and the coffee tang what dad loved. Holly Lock is scented as new crop blackberries. When I feel strong in voice I move in closeness to her and she hears and looks with surprise signs up on her.

I stumble to force the birth day words out into the air between us and she does not look so scared up as past time. I tell of my gift in one gush.

'Why are you talking to me? Why have you got me a present?' she asks, but the voice in her is not with full anger so I am encouraged on.

When I tell of it as secret and for surprise I do see interest and I say she must follow my steppings to have knowledge of it.

'Why should I?' she says but her eyes do not immediate look past for escape.

Within my watchings in past times I noticed kiddypigs telling 'scaredycat' when they had want of other kiddypigs doing a thing, so I struggle to make these wordshapes for Holly. I think they do come out too strangely for her understanding.

'What d'you want? Why are you hassling me?' she says.

I tell that she is a special one and she looks immediate worried and then I cannot find correct wordings for explanation.

'Why am I special? I don't understand.'

Far back up on the wide road what smells of chips and engine oils, my lop ears hear other kiddypigs lurching about. They will plod for the woods soon, some want to make the dare game to come here. I tell Holly to follow for my special place, I tell that there is pleasure there. The words I make are half strangled up but she grabs them good.

'Don't come any closer, Jack Plum,' she says extreme serious.

I make the promise of keeping distance, crossing fingers in front side of heart, which is bamming like the woodpecker does.

I lead for the spot where long, straggled garden cusps wood and do not look back but have knowing that she follows on my steps. I press away shrubbery to uncloak my builded door. Made by me when mam made the threats to block up my cellar inside door. My pig door, within the woods is reached only from inside the Palace, for extra safeness. I do not want kiddypigs figuring a way in with scorching tempers and wickedness.

'Where are you going?' Holly asks. There is the quiver in her voice.

I make explanation of the downsteps up on hog hands, six in number, and how she must go firstly but she will not take this and tells I must take the leading down.

When I open the downdoor I hear piggywigs breathe extra soft, they wait for the meet with Holly, for the smell of her. I have told about her and of my pigrelic wishing. Some piggylets begin a pattering and Holly hears this.

'There's something down there,' she says, 'I can hear things moving. What is it, what's down there?'

I make my voice extreme soft for not scaring and say of the good surprise what waits for her.

Just as I think she is far from the fear, she twirls like sheep chased by worrisome canines, up through garden, out into road, where other kiddypigs slouch and wait for happenings. I am slowly at my street gate and there within the midst of them, she leans, snatching at breath, seeing me below the eyelashes. One kiddypigboy, Colin, takes notice of me and makes the loud oomphing noises.

'Freak alert!' he shouts. 'Freak alert!'

Others join the noises and Colin kiddypigboy is brave, with eyes all up on him, he runs at my space, jittering arms and head like one without muscle connectors. Far and low within me is the small knobbly anger place what I have known before this time. Partly I want it to grow huge and blaring, partly I want it to go to nothing. Sensibleness wins and I turn off and insidedoors. Stones crackle at walls and fence, warnings to the Freak to keep off the outside in daylightime.

Mam is deadly drunk in the wheelchair, slumped as a half-used sack of meal, in two pouches. The stinging smell tells that her nappy is bad soiled and I must pinch my nose and stall the breath to make the changes. She fights at me with the lift to the sofa, punching and pinching and slithering out words on her lost beauty and men what queued to dance with her. I believe this story is a true one as way below the bitterness lines and anger scars up on her face, I see handsomeness. And in sleeptime her skin is gentle, her mouth is not pulled so much to the earth, and I know why dad loved her in past times. I love her also, though not as he did, and would like love back from her. Though I can admit to disgustingness times as now, when the nappy is packed and leaking through edges and stinks as Farmer Cotton's bad tended sewage pile. And she makes much spit at my hogcheek as I swab her to cleanness.

After she is wiped and dried and nappied back up I hutch her up on my back and upsteps to bed, covering the quilt in to her chin. She grabs at me with the wrinkly arms to keep me in close.

'Stay with me, Jack my too-big lad,' she slurps. 'Stay with me and whistle sweetly until I forget about everything real. Stay with me.'

I do stay and make whistling. These are tender moments what fill me up for those too many times she turns the hate at me. I whistle all tunes I know, tumble them one on the other until tiny grunts say she is gone into the dreamplace of better times, without me in the picture. I watch the pucked face and trembly eyes and make an imagining that dad is in her dreamtime. I close my lids to try and make pictures of them together in tenderness which would be before my hatching. Life air is on my lips as I breathe time a way, and there, in mam's unhappy space, I think on all the outsideworld pulling and pushing lifebreath in and out and all that air mingling. All of us, everywhere, swapping the breath. Then I go in extreme quiet to my pigs, brothers and sisters under the skin and I dwell on Holly Lock and how I did not make the connection and I listen long to pigsong for my answers.

FOUR

Holly Lock's world

When I went into the woods again today it was almost like I had to dare myself, to prove that I could handle it. Mrs Dove was talking about it in English last week, how she thinks people read scary books and watch horror films as a sort of rehearsal for life, almost to prepare themselves for awful stuff that might happen. I thought it was a really sound idea but Colin had to butt in as usual, he said that's why he read porn magazines, to prepare himself for the real thing. Mrs Dove was quick though, she said she was glad to hear he was still a virgin and all the other lads fell about laughing.

He's a strange mixture, Colin. He's tall and slim with really thick black hair but he uses that much gel it drips down the side of his face like his hair's sweating. His clothes are crap, cheap sports, baseball cap and trainers which look as if they've had a mud bath. When he's on his own with me he's sort of quiet and thoughtful and I can tell that he does think about the stuff we do at school. But most of the time he's with his mates being loud and bossy and you wouldn't think he had a brain at all.

Anyway, I didn't see why I should stop going in Pardes Wood, just because Jack Plum went there, it's my favourite place and I'd never find a ghost orchid if I backed off. Also, there was something about seeing Jack Plum through my bedroom window in the early hours of the morning, getting on with his weird and separate life, that sort of fascinated me. Samantha and Colin and that lot can be so boring when they're all together. They won't go in the woods unless it's a proper dare, all they ever want to do is hang out, drinking and smoking, and playing the dare game is just an excuse for snogging. Not that I care but the lads always want to kiss Samantha because she's got breasts and wears a bra. The other day she told me she's got pubes as well now and I thought that was tacky, to tell someone, and then Colin started boasting about his and that was enough for me. The other girls round here are either a lot younger than me or a lot older, which is probably why Samantha's always hanging round me. It's hard to make friends at school, most of them think I'm weird because I'm not obsessed by lads or make-up or designer clothes. Imagine what they'd think if they knew I liked plants and went searching for them in the woods.

I like being on my own anyway and Pardes Wood is the perfect place. None of the others like going there by themselves because our parents have always told us to keep away, like it's cursed or something. According to Grandma Logan 'pard' is an old name for leopard and there were rumours of a leopard pack living deep inside the woods when she was a kid.

Nobody I know has ever been inside Jack Plum's house and I don't remember ever seeing his mam and dad. I heard Colin say that Mrs Plum made Jack by having sex with Farmer Cotton's bull, and that's how he got his big head. But then Colin would say something like that.

When I saw Jack Plum again, close up, I got that rushing feeling you get when you wish you hadn't done something but you can't take it back. I noticed how he kept his head and eyes down, like he was frightened to face me, so I moved a bit nearer. His small eyes were watery but very bright and very blue. There were little beads of spittle at the corners of his mouth which he wiped at all the time with a big red hanky. When I didn't get angry or run off, his grin came right across his face. His teeth were very white and even.

Mam said he'd never done anything bad but I'm not stupid and you hear of those disgusting men who fancy young girls and want to have sex with them. Mam's always going on about it when she sees me on the internet. And I have gone into some chat rooms, to see what they were like but it's not for me, I like to see who I'm talking too, I like to watch their faces and check what they do with their hands. Body language, that's another of Mrs Dove's things.

She told us that the police have all these gestures that they look for when they're interviewing a suspect, like if they touch their face or hair a lot. Who works all these things out?

Jack Plum was very still. He just said his stuff then waited. He knew I could shout or run and tell mam that he was bothering me but he still took the risk. Part of me really wanted to know why he kept trying to talk to me, and why he wanted to give me a present. Another part of me was a bit flattered as well, that he'd picked me to talk to, me, out of all the people he could have picked, like Samantha for instance. But I wasn't ready to go down those dark steps.

Mam says I'm growing up but actually I know she's worried because I'm so far behind the other girls in my class. Most of them have started their periods and have got breasts and waists but I'm still flat and straight. Dodgy hormones, she says, trying to keep it light. I'm clever though. Always near the top of the class in SATS. Mrs Dove says she expects me to excel in my GCSEs.

Saturday's always video night with mam. Her turn to choose the film. I got popcorn, chocolate, a tiny glass of wine out of her bottle, and the film took my mind off Jack Plum. Later, mam chose 'The High Priestess' from the tarot. This is a holy woman seated on a throne holding a large book with a crescent moon by her feet. There is a column on either side of her, one with the letter B on it and one with the letter J.

'This card encourages you to use your intuition when you have to make an important decision,' mam said. 'It tells you to listen to your heart more than your head.'

When I thought about it, I realised that I made decisions by listening to both. Sometimes one was stronger than the other, and sometimes they really contradicted one another.

Settled in my bedroom, I brought my lemon geranium next to the bed so the scent of it would be close all night long. Lying there, mulling it all over, I knew my head was telling me to keep away from Jack Plum but my heart was saying the opposite. It wanted me to take risks, it told me Pardes Wood was my place just as much as it was anyone else's. I'd never paid much attention to the tarot before, just gone through the motions with mam, but it did seem to be communicating with me. How bloody weird, that a pack of cards with pictures on could actually mean something. Before I went to sleep I couldn't resist peeping out into the street, half-hoping to see Jack Plum out and about. No sign, though.

FIVE

In which a piggylet is named

Last night came wild with boisterous wind. I did not go tromping the darktime roads or any where by Holly Lock's place. She saw me that time gone before and I could feel worries coming from her. Early daylight time I fetch dropped down beech nuts for my pigs. They love the bruisy sweetness and chomping is of benefit for them. All come at their names when I make the calls and if I make songs they buck about as broncos, dancing their especial pigdance, bumping me to join and become like the grizzly bear with fleas. Even piggylets do this bump dance.

I talk with them on Holly Lock as they lollop the water and dig hollow bedshapes in the sandy ground to cool down in. They know of my curiosity for Holly, my desiring to have the friend of my own humanpig kind. This day I will try hardest to make her take trust. The pigs understand they must have full stillness when she approaches by and they will be of help in this. Freya will see it is just so.

Mam waked up by four this a.m. She had the melancholics after dreaming her legs were brought good again and she said the hurting things about wanting to slice me into rashers when I was hogboy little.

'Sometimes I'd take a razor blade and run it along your neck,' she telled. 'Right along the skin, making a fine red line, and you'd wriggle and kick like a tapeworm until I fastened you tight in your blanket so that you could barely breathe. Of course, your pigheaded father always loosened you off. He used to tell me I was insane. Me! Huh! You've no idea of the life I had with that swine.'

On and on she went, pinning me at the spot with that vengeful eye, to make full sure I knew, an other time more, of the horror things I fetched to her. Sometimes, when it is extreme early, still darkness in the outsideworld, and all pigs full asleep, mam's words snap at me like springy barbed stuff and I plan of putting this fat head within dustbinbags and fastening tight so that all things end. And some times, in the very dark time and she's very whiskymean, I think to lash at her and fetch silence to the sourness. Only some times.

Holly Lock puts me in memory time of an angel what I saw in a churchyard one past time when dad fetched me to rub the brasses. He had his friend what called at our house – this was time before mam stopped her outside visits – and it was a schooltime friend. Murg was his calledby name and some early times, right by sunup, he would tootaroot out the side of my window. His motoring bike had a side-cart on for taking me and dad swung up on behind Murg. Then we would tumult off to rub the brass things in churches and places and taste sweetcakes and fizzing drinks in between times. We could be out days long and mam would be cruelly angry and extra at Murg who she had proper hates for. And this angel of stone was overlooking the buried place of a baby, and it had this blossomy smile. Dad telled me of the words there written and it was of cherubs and no harm to come in paradise and that face of the angel was of some thing in Holly Lock.

Later, within the daylight time, I see her lurk about with that Samantha. I tell to my pigs a new wishing thing about if Holly does come to Pardes Wood before the six p.m. I will know the sign is of purpose to talk with her again. Then I wait, silent as fresh snowflakes on a far unwaked field, close aside trees at my trapdoor, and she does come and before the appointed timing.

This time of coming she still makes argues and runs off away firstly but one half hour later she creeps back and we gets her feet up on the top step to dip down to Pig Palace before she holds it back. I tell her all is good, nothing to give fright. I give her my best rubber torch what dad gave for my nine birth days. Small fingers press at the fat button and she goes on down the steps. She stops after only some seconds to shine this torch direct at my face, though Freya has every piggylet in silent time. There is a tremble about her lips and her eyes do have a glimmer of frighteners up on them. I make a stumble on the downstep for the upset I give to her which is not within my wishing.

'I want to go home now,' she says in fierceness. 'Please get out of my way.' I is heart-heavy and full with enormous sighs what wave up from my feet, but I will not give her more frights, so I move for her to pass away. But, she turns the torch back downward, and her breath pulls in through her teeth and I know she is not so feared.

The pigs are in difficulty with full stillness when they smell at and see of Holly, and she shines the light up on them.

'Pigs?' she says with her feet plopping on to my soft earth floor. 'Pigs?'

And there it is, the wondering surprises within her voice, just as I had the guess it would be. And laced up within I hear the frights still as what she comes up on here is extreme strange to her. I switch for the majorlight and turn it, for her to gather the whole picture of Pig Palace.

'Piggy wig wiggy pig wiggies,' I say. 'Jack's pigs, Jack Plum's porkers!'

And she gives a long, long, piano laugh as the piggylets atwirl up on her feet and Freya rubs close at her legs with grunts to welcome and tell all sounder crew of this acceptance. Holly Lock turns bright eyes over me and gives more and more laughing until I think her breath will halt. And she walks at all the spaces and stares and gawps long and touches flowers and ornament stuff like it is Alice in the wonder land.

'Who made this place, Jack Plum? Where did the pigs come from? Who looks after them?' she questions all in one scoop.

'Me, me and me!' I say. 'Dad started . . . before . . . he was gone . . . he loved pigs . . . Jack finished it . . . get first pigs at Farmer Cotton's fields.'

'But that's stealing, Jack,' she says.

'I give back Holly . . . lots more . . . than borrowed . . . good breeder, swap pigs.'

'And Farmer Cotton doesn't know?'

'No, does not know.'

She laughs more and I join with her, and keep my boomy laugh soft so as not to worry. There is a lifting of something up off my heart, a lighteningness, even the hoghead is less of weight. My words come out easy, making the good shapes for her.

'You've stopped stuttering, Jack Plum,' she says in wiseness, and I know the rightness in the choosing of Holly Lock to share Pig Palace world. I nod my hoghead and tell of the happiness with pigs what helps brain and mouth work together. And she asks for the full tale of the coming of Pig Palace and listens entire to all the words, even the ones I still break and at the ending of it there is her big smile, the electric light one what comes full on.

'That's just incredible,' she says. 'You can really talk properly and you've made all of this and you breed your pigs and no one's ever found out. I can't believe it.'

I make explanation of how I choosed her from all others to become pigfriend and my friend. She is much pleasured on that but wants knowledge of all the 'why' things. Why her, and why keep secret for long time past without the telling? And I describe on the alone space within her what I do see even though she does pomp and tribe about. I say also of my own alone space what I did have need of sharing.

When she is still in some questionings I give extra much time to tell about aloneness as okay, like dad told to me but that it might turn to lone liness which makes for anger turnedin, like mam. I know from her face shapes that I make a connecting and complete within I think words like 'destiny' what are to do with luck and wishes on pigrelic stone and stars in dark time skies. I speak long stretches of words as never before and my tongue comes full loose as if oiled.

Freya rubs the wet snout up on Holly's arm, this makes a full sanctioning, allowing of her to be aside new piggylets. Freya is elder of my pig cluster as well as sounder mam, what she accepts, they do accept.

'Freya likes you, welcomes you,' I tell Holly. She strokes on top of Freya's head and backs of her ears, like a canine thing, and Freya and all others make big snorts and guzzles.

'Where did your dad go, Jack?' Holly asks then.

When I make the head shakes she looks to me with sadness sparks on her eyes so I tell I do not like to dwell up on dad and his leaving or the empty space where he occupied once. And she does speak soft on how her dad did leave also and I get surprised and filled of warm that she does make a connection with alone places and the absence of dads, for this is up on my thoughts all times.

I did choose good with Holly Lock and I wish so much to be able to speak words out at her as I mould them within the hoghead, to show who really lives inside this gobliny shape. But for the now, I get happy as I have been ever. It is like dream time in the place you love of most. And I must make the gift so I search among the piggylets and select one to give Holly. I do it with ceremony thoughts within and thanking thoughts to the pigrelicstone, as is the way for things.

'For Holly. Happy birth day, here, take,' I say.

She takes the wriggling piggylet and rests it close at her heart, the wide smile full of gurgles. 'Ooh, it's so gorgeous. Is it really mine? Can I really keep it?'

'Yes. I will take care and show how to you if you visit more.'

'Try and stop me,' she says with much strokes on piggylet.

'And it must be fully secret,' I tell.

'It'll be our secret.'

'Promise?' I say for ritual.

'Cross my heart and hope to die. Ouch! It nibbled me.'

Piggylet is filled of hunger for the mam's milk so I do take it from Holly with much gentleness to place it close up on Freya and the other piggybabes for feedtime. They shuffle and wriggle to discover their own teats, the ones what they did claim early. A loud snuffling grunting crams the air as they gobble. Holly stares, kneeling beside, eyes full of unexpectedness.

'Freya is so huge, Jack! I've never seen such a large pig.'

'Good pig, eight piggylets this time. Have piggylets two times a year.'

I pull fresh hay for Holly to sit. She smiles and pats at the space by her. 'Come and sit down, Jack, tell me about the pigs. How long does their carrying take? Y'know, like humans take nine months.'

I sit, but not in closeness. I leave space enough for some cat to curl between us. I know of the importance that I keep distance, me being so big and untidy next her. And I make explanation of my learning on pigs, on gestation what is called Farrowing and is filled of strangeness, for it does take three months, three weeks and three days. This I believe is extreme special and I do see on Holly's face her full joy at this knowing.

Some of the piggylets is gobbled full now. They roll from Freya and stumble at the small waterfall and pond, rollicking and splashing like ducklets. Holly watches and gives more laughing. I like it, this laugh, it says freedom, it says she will have the whole world full ahead of her and nothing to impede.

'They like water then?' she says, as they shake out near by her legs.

I say on pigs not having sweatglands and that is the love of water in them, to make cool on the skin, and that is reasoning they make rolls within mud if no water is near by. Not on account of being dirty beasts but in necessity of cooling blood system.

'You are clever, Jack Plum, to know all this stuff. Oh, look, is that my piglet? Has it come back to me?' I nod the hoghead slow and Holly catches the pigbabe up. 'Look at its eyes, Jack, so sharp, so bright, just as if it's thinking.'

When I tell of pig thinking and extreme intelligence she puts even more questions at me, so I say of an other sense they do have what I name 'pigsense'. This gives them the knowing of moods and changes within pigs and humanpigs and all spaces in and about them. Like they is connected to all things around and their bristles is the bringer of signals.

'They're not as clever as dogs, though, are they?'

This is the thought in much of the outsideworld but I give knowledge of how pigs is much cleverer. I tell of what me and dad heard on radio one time, a challenging thing for pig scientifics and chimpmonkey scientifics. Holly makes the word 'contest' and this I recall is correct. A contest of pigs and chimpmonkeys where they did make especial testings and puzzles and problem fathoming and all overlooked by scientifics judge people and all of two full daytimes to carry through. She is total wrapped in this idea and when I make knowledge that the pigs did win this contesting, we is both loosed up with happiness. And I make my exciting times jump and Holly enjoins with fat smiles and high chortles and all the pigs gather and stomp about in turbulence until we fall on the hay stackings with great breathings. And when it is calm again I say she must name the piggylet.

She thinks for some while, turning her head thisthat way. 'Peter,' she says, 'Peter pig.' I let out my full roaring thunderstorm laugh and make her jump. I see the sudden rushing fear in her sharp eyes, then it does exit, quick as it arrived.

'Girl piglet, Holly . . . girl!' I say.

'Girl, oh, okay . . . so . . . Penny? . . . No, that's not right . . . Poppy? . . . No, Peach! That's it, Jack . . . Jack Plum, Peach pig.' And Holly's face does come to beam with smiles.

That is when mam starts the banging stick and the shouting of me. Holly takes worry into her face and I do tell of it being mam within the wheel chair and wanting of assistance and then she is in full understanding. She says she must depart also and I do feel the small beginnings of losing her again to the outside world. When she makes questions on how to visit with us more I get filled of joy as she will return.

I explain we have to be extreme careful that no kiddypigs find the Palace and she tells how she can not let it come known, that it is unallowed to see me, so we make the pact, her titchy hand up on my jumbo one. And I show to her the extra key space and where rubber torch lives and I survey that no kiddypigs is out and about before she clambers into the wood and the outsideworld.

Back down to the Palace I carry a sadness dollop up on my stomach, heavy as a stone, because there is the knowing that me and Holly Lock can never be out in the open friends. Freya and the other pigs comprehend my droopiness and cluster me silently, pressing warmth to make me safe. Mam's banging stick starts up again and I put my blue dismals aside and go to her.

SIX

Holly Lock's world

Sometimes when I'm watching a really frightening film on TV I want to run out of the room because it's too much to take. When I was standing on the steps down to Jack's Palace, with him behind me and the darkness below, I got the same feeling. My heart was juddering too much and my mouth was dry as dust. But in the torchlight his eyes looked so gentle I took a chance. And it was like Mrs Dove said, by facing it I realised I could overcome the fear. As soon I saw the pigs, I knew it was all okay. He didn't want to frighten me or hurt me, he just wanted to show me his pigs, he wanted to share his secret with someone and he'd chosen me.

There was this music at junior school, our PE teacher Miss Judd used to play it for movement lessons. *In the Hall of the Mountain King*, it was called. It used to scare me and make me feel excited all at the same time. And as I looked around Jack's amazing creation it just popped into my head. It was perfect because it summed up exactly how I felt. The waterfall, the bells, the artificial grass and flowers, the little handmade pens full of fresh hay and the troughs, all with pictures of pigs painted on them, and the hay bales stretching right up to the ceiling. It's a magical place, Jack is the King and he's invited me into his pigdom.

It's amazing how he lives this completely separate life, all hidden away, doings things in the night when everyone else is sleeping, breeding his pigs and swapping them. It's the sort of thing you read about in books but you never think will happen to you. That's what I was looking for in Pardes Wood, for something unusual to happen. And the thing is I have to keep it secret, because that's the whole point of it. Jack doesn't want anyone else to know. I can carry it round inside my head and dip into it whenever I want and best of all I can go there, get away from everything, be hidden away with Jack and Peach and all the other pigs. How can I eat bacon and sausage and chops now that Jack's told me pigs are more intelligent than chimps? I'll have to go full veggie or else I'll have to explain why it's just pigs I don't want to eat.

I'd love to find out what Jack's dad was like. It was his idea to build the Palace and get the pigs so he must have been an unusual guy. Don't remember much about mine except maybe the damp, oily smell he used to have on his clothes. Mam said it was from working on cars all day long. I do remember he had a squeaky type of voice and when he shouted it really did my head in, it sounded sort of mechanical and he shouted quite a lot. Nothing ever seemed to please him. Can't picture him with a smile on his face or taking me out or reading to me, nothing like that. Just the oily smell, the squeakiness and the bad temper.

As it was getting dark I looked out of my window towards Pardes Wood. Jack told me he took the pigs there at night, into the deepest part, where the river is. Samantha and Colin were at the end of our garden, smoking. She waved at me to come out but I pretended I hadn't seen her. I wasn't in the mood for her chattering. She just smokes for effect because she reckons it's cool. She doesn't inhale the way Colin does, right down to his boots, and I've sometimes seen her nose wrinkle up at the first few drags, as if she's forcing herself to do it. She's always got to have the hottest gear as well, as if it's some sort of religion, and she wears loads of make-up. Mrs Dove's always telling her to go and wash her face and give her skin a chance to breathe. Thing is, she's actually got gorgeous skin, naturally tan with apricot-coloured cheeks, and lips and teeth just like Julia Roberts. I hate it if she stands next to me in the toilets at school when I'm brushing my hair. It's like Cinderella and her ugly little sister. My skin is pink and full of freckles and I've got really thick eyebrows. And when she stares at me with this wary look she has, I sometimes can't tell whether Samantha likes me or hates me.

When Samantha went off, Colin hung about by our gate. I saw him glance up the path once or twice as if he was hoping I'd go out. But when I do hang out with him he behaves like an arsehole. Like the other day, at school, he told one of the other lads, Trevor Quilling, that he'd got 'animal magnetism'. I nearly choked trying not to laugh out loud. He thinks it means not washing or changing his duds every day. He thinks that's why some lasses like bikers, because they smell of oil and stuff. What an idiot.

Don't know why Trevor listens to him because he's far more interesting than Colin. He likes books for a start, asks good questions in English. His clothes are ace and he looks a bit like Hugh Grant only not so self absorbed. But he lives at the other end of Jesmond Dene so I never see him out of school and anyway, I reckon he'd never fancy me, I don't look much older than his sister and she's in Year 6.

Jack Plum thinks I'm special though. If he'd been interested in somebody pretty he would have picked Samantha not me but he said he knew I was clever and would love his pigs, he could tell from watching me. And when he's with the pigs and he stops stuttering I can tell that he's clever as well. Everything he knows and everything he's built he wants to share with me and he doesn't give a damn about breasts and stuff like that.

Mam was late home tonight and she'd forgotten to get my favourite bolognese sauce for the spaghetti. Then she was on the phone for ages, I could hear the rumble of her voice through my bedroom wall. When I went downstairs for the tarot ritual she was very quiet and I thought she was going to tell me something important, like Gran was ill, but she didn't. Instead she asked me to pick a card. I selected 'The Hanged Man'. The picture shows a man hanging from a tree by his left foot. The other leg is folded behind, making a cross shape and his arms are behind his back, like they might be tied. He has a halo around his head.

'It's telling you to be prepared to look at a situation from a new perspective, not just to think what it means to you, but to see the best for everyone concerned,' mam explained. For some reason this card seemed to please her, almost as if she'd wanted me to pick it. Very strange.

In my bedroom, one of the flowers from my slipper orchid had fallen on the floor. It looked like an exotic butterfly resting on my dark green carpet. I pressed it between tissue paper and put it in the orchid section of my flower book.

Grandad Logan gave me some old cigarette cards before he left, said they'd become 'collector's items' and make me some money one day. They're in sets and depict different subjects such as footballers, cars and so on. One set is all flowers, they're beautiful, fold-over cards with embroidered pictures on the inside. The one with a slipper orchid has the name 'Lady's Slipper', and it says that in France and Portugal they call it 'Shoe of the Virgin'. Years and years back they used to make a drink from the petals, an elixir, which was supposed to cure epilepsy.

SEVEN

Whisky time

When I get upsteps mam drones as an angry bee does if trapped aside a closed up window. Buzzing and cursing irritation and all of my fault as is usual.

'What did I do to deserve you, eh?' she says, rat tat tatting up on the lino with the stick.

'I . . . I . . .' I try, but words fly off, flutter into absence, leaving me with spit and splutter. My tongue is massive big and blocking across the throat.

'Shut up! Just shut up!' she says, her voice a gravelling cough and spots of blood land all up on her blouse. 'Stop blubbering,' mam goes on, 'and fetch the towel, that one, you clown!' More blood comes chugging with more coughs. I try and wipe at her with tissues but she splats away at me. 'Don't touch me,' she crackles, 'I can't bear it when you touch me.'

She lunges across her face with the towel what always sits up on her knees, trying to lash me and then slumps back with a harsh sighing. 'I'm going to die,' she says, 'alone, watched over by a mumbling, hideous gargoyle . . . why? Why me?'

Not a thing can be levered from within my mouth. I am feared of the blood, and of the talk of death and a trembling comes across me, a iciness. Mam barks sharp things out her mouth. They is to make hurt on me, as the stick would if she might reach. It is all about how she wanted me birthed dead, that it was meant to be that way, and then more of it on how my hatching did bring destructions on her life.

My hands have the full shakes at her nasties and I crush the first glass in my hoghand and as I gather at the pieces she laughs at the blood spurts and tries for splatting me with her stick.

'Water!' she yells out and I towel up my hand and fetch a new glass with water to her. She drinks it all down like there is no time to come, and slops driblets up on her clothes.

'They'll take you away when I'm dead,' she says. 'They'll lock you up and throw away the key.'

I cannot squeeze a sound through sand dry lips but I do shake the hoghead swift to almost dizzy time as she tells how I do deserve such punishments for my damage of her, for prisoning her within the wheelchair. Which dad telled I did not have the doing of as she did walk many years on from my hatch.

'Hardly able to walk, hardly a life at all, and a swine of a husband who gave me an ugly boar and didn't stay around for more. Whisky! I need more whisky.'

I make explanation how I will collect it later times, when the kiddypigs is not plotting about and welcoming trouble. But she will not hear of my words and does make insistence on me going for whisky straight off. And when I makes hesitance she does start the bloodcoughing again, more so, and I know I must venture within kiddypig territory before the cover of darktime falls to fetch her whisky comfort.

I put on my special hat to try and hide the hoghead. Dad made it from an old leather coat. It covers my lop ears and dips deep around the chin. I have worries the look is as an executioner from olden days, like in pictures I have seen. But better to try and cover the big boar bonce than flaunt.

I have mam's note and purse in one hand, with the canvas bag for whisky within the other. I believe that hands full seem less worrysome to outside people. I never look direct to anyone's eyes, that is learned from my pigs. Purpose full eye contact is as a daring when it does come from an unfriended beast like me and I have no desire to greet conflict. My very own shadow pulsing up on the ground is enough to fetch fears to most.

At my gate I wait to check up on the street. No sign of kiddy pigs, no scent of them, no sound of them. Perhaps they are chomping on dinners or riding the Metro without ticketing. That is my hope. I have the long stretch of houses with watching windows, then the sharp corner at the right before I am able to look up on the shop what sells nearly everything a house might need. I move hastily as my hoghead will allow, eyes below, whispering wishes that I meet not one.

Half the way into the stretch I get the smell of kiddypigboys. They is hidden and waiting as they have done times past and I do fear the spitefulness of them, the way they look to me as beast and Freak, for they could fetch the outsideworld full in at me to crush my Palace into dust and bloodiness.

I stumble to the far pavestones, to put distance on us, but there is Colinkiddypig boy sliding without a gate and he spreads himself across my direction. He has the bat within his hand, with its sway from side to side as if it climbs a long arc, like someone working themselves on a parkswing. I step to the road middle where I see the kiddypigboys lining in a ridge holding on sticks so I must move within them. I contemplate on returning back but mam's anger and needness engines me on. I dwell on thoughts of my pigs and that gives me up the strength of love.

The kiddypigboys all have sticks of some brand and as I get to near by I smell excitement up on them and fear as they begin the chant of their own taunt words.

'Keep the Freaks off the street . . . keep the Freaks off the street.'

Each time they speak the 'keep' word they hit at me, legs, back, high as they are able. None are big enough to get up on my pigskull and I am grate full at that. I do not cry. I do not look. I say these words within my hoghead and they roll round and round like bagatelle balls on the wooden game dad found. I slouch on, biting at the pain, pressing teeth inside my lips. I limp bad as I have rounded the shop corner. I most likely bleed below my clothes because of this hogskin of me being extreme thin like new born piggylets, it does split and bruise extra easy.

Within the shop Mrs Robson tries the niceness as is usual but I see the tremor when she looks at these shovel hands. She thinks of the damage what hands like these could do. I want to say my uglies is outside only for reassuring her but cannot. She wraps mam's whisky within news paper and plops it in my bag so it is snug. I remember the dozens and dozens of whisky bottles I have fetched from here over long years. Maybe thousands now, and all gone within mam and out that other end, and all empty bottles left for dustbin days.

Mrs Robson counts the change money extra slow because she thinks I have no brain machinery at all. I do not speak, strangled sounds would fright her more than none. When I do move to leave, my head is full of the worry of kiddypigboys and if they will be in wait. They know I go never further than this shop. I can not see Holly Lock and her mam coming in at me so the door smacks at my sore knees and I crumble in my middle, and when I look up I am staring full at Mrs Lock's face. She makes a tiny gasp but then tries to smile and Holly holds the door extra wide for my escape. As I go I give a sideways peep and

Holly's mouth does a turn up at the corners and I am much better, much more in and of the world.

The kiddypigboys wait up on the corner, carelessly leaning thisthat way. When I shuffle on they stand straight, ready for more bruising. I hear into their whisperings and grasp they want mam's whisky but I can not allow it because her need is great. They raise up their hitting sticks and I lift my body up tall, stretch my hoghead high and I roar as a massive boar would do. The noise is extreme louder than any one could imagine because it is dragged up from the very deeps of my stomach and hurled at the air. Those kiddypigboys not frozen to their spots, run. They call out, back over shaky shoulders, 'Freak, Freak, Freak,' as a sort of charm of magic, for a pretend they have no frights.

At home, mam takes no notice of my hurts, she has no desires to give comfort to her gargoyle. She makes the grab for whisky and that nobble of anger in me starts a surge, like I might plod the damned bottle on her hating skull and smash all to nothingness. This raging makes my hogheart crash and wallop and I see spots on the eyeballs, but some other inmost place whispers at me that I am carrying pain from the kiddypigboys into mam, turning it at her and that is what lashing is made of. Mam reads something of this in me and makes a reach at her stick that she can beat me away. I give out the bottle and make distance from her.

After she has the hold of her whisky she settles into TV

things and I am free to visit with my pigs. I lay frontways, flat up on the hay and with sharp hurting breaths, I tell of the kiddypigboys stuff. The pigs lick at my hurts with raspy tongues and clamber over me, rubbing and nuzzling until they know I am in calm.

Up on the next day, after schooltime, Holly Lock comes back to visit, and I am filled up with a great prospect of this as an every day thing to come. The pigs is washed and they run at her to rub wetness up on her legs. Her laugh comes as our waterfall, gurgly and flowing. Far deep within is a warm place what Holly Lock touches. I give dad's old butcher coat to keep her clothes clean and show the dry and oil of Peach pig and I try to keep my damages from her eyes.

'Rub oil in all over then sprinkle this,' I tell, and she sneezes loud, one, two, three. 'Jupiter protect,' I say with the snap of fingers.

'What's that for?' she asks.

'Dad said it stops the soul 'scaping the body from through the mouth.'

'Where is your dad, Jack? Won't you tell me?'

She is full of the questions which is as should be, I think. They are questions deserving of answers, not just the snoop kind.

'Gone . . . long time, my fault. Too ugly, head too empty . . . so, Holly, you do sprinkle –' and she sneezes again, which makes extra laughs for us both. The pigs love this laughing and they stomp their hooves and snortle.

'What's that stuff, Jack, the stuff that makes me sneeze?' I see she lets go of the dad and I am pleased. It will be a later talk thing for us maybe.

I explain of the powdered sawdust and its goodness for porkers' skin. She holds at her nose, pours into Peach's skin and rubs until the piggylet almost sings for pleasure.

I wave out my big arm and tell Holly that all of the Palace is her secret place now. I see pleasure in her as she wanders into corners, curious eyes seeking, hands all loose at her back. Peach follows on, running in and over her legs and sidestepping her toes. All the pigs murmur soft, offering the true sharing of their homespace.

'It was weird seeing you in the shop yesterday,' Holly says. 'When we're down here it's like the rest of the world has stopped and we're not any part of it, then bumping into you up there . . .' Her words slither off and she stares to me, needing me to name it. Which I do as it is much necessary. I tell how I is Freak in the outsideworld and when she makes head shakes I say I know the truth of it, how it has been so for long enough. They are not Freak but I am. I am Freak to all and I make explanation how she is to be with their side of things on the upoutside. It's the way. Other wise trouble does brew so she must never look up on me as friend upoutside or they will place her along at me and call her Freak also.

I wave my arms awkwardly as windmills when I talk out

to make expressions for her and she sees the hurts and rushes to me. I move sideways from her but she makes me bend low for her to see.

'Who did this to you, Jack? Tell me? Tell me who hurt you? Was it your mam?' she asks.

I do the head shake. I wish not to tell of the badness of pigboys but she is forceful for knowing. And after wards she hangs her head and is very downcast.

'You can't let them get away with this, Jack. You could bash their bloody skulls in. I would if I was you. I'd give them a really good kicking.'

I tell that it would not be good way. I am very certain and loud in my voice.

'They're bastards, Jack, I hate them!' she says with full fury.

Then she gives me up a dumpy smile but I see a confused thing at what she feels. I decide to change moodiness and show the clever thing I do with my voice. I want her to know the all of me. I sing in best highness and chuck the sound up on different corners of the Palace so Holly is twisting this way that and her eyes fill with questionings.

'Jack!' she says. 'Who is that singing?'

I say it is the pigs firstly but she does not believe me so I sing at the corners and bring my voice back within my throat for her understanding, like this:

> The time has come, the Walrus said,
> To talk of many things.

Of shoes – and ships – and sealing wax –
Of cabbages – and Kings.

She can not believe, she stares and stares and I sing some more:

And why the sea is boiling hot
And whether pigs have wings

'Jack Plum, it is you!' she says, filled full with the delight. 'That's amazing. D'you think you could teach me how to do it?'

It was showed to dad by a big sailorcaptainman one long time back and I do not know the possibility of Holly making learning of it because dad did always say it was my big neck and head and the big . . . wobbly bits what let me do it so good. He could not make it sound any ways but she is in such wanting we do make a try. Her face comes screwed with the determination and she puts big efforts in but ends with the sore throat and stumbly cough. I know her disappointment insideoutside and my hoghead is sorry. She walks slow around the Palace to push down her fedupness and before long times Peach has the smile coming up with her grunting gambolling.

She sees of my radio in one corner and makes a point at it. 'Why d'you listen to this station? It's all talk and you could get a music channel, shall I show you?'

I shake the hoghead and tell when dad showed how to listen on the words and how it does give me new knowings of the outsideworld – much what I do not like and not make an understanding of – but how also I gets the meanings on extra words to take and remember and keep inside the hogbrain for use.

Then she does stop by my especial cupboard of books and stuff so I show where to press for the door to open. She says again of my cleverness to build lovely things and I am swanked up with the pride of it. That was dad's word of looking and feeling extra good – swanky – and I do like the sound it makes. I tell how dad read to me, how he gathered all books he could with pigs in. She makes a giggle and picks them one by one, speaking the names out. *Animal Farm*, *The Tale of Pigling Bland*, *Padre Porko*, *The Three Little Pigs* . . .

'"I'll huff and I'll puff and I'll . . ."' she says.

'" . . . blow your house down",' I say and then I ask if she will make the reading to me and pigs.

When she says the yes, the pigs snort and squeal with the excitement as they know I am filled up with delight and for some seconds, there is hullabaloo in the Palace, like never before. I pass one of the *Winnie the Pooh* books and settle within a huddle of the pigs, as a belly-god with piglings all over, and she begins the read 'In which Piglet does a Very Grand Thing'. Her voice is full with sweetness, as plum pudding and soon I am there at that 'Thoughtful Spot' with Pooh and Piglet and captured up in their dilemmas of what to do with time, until Holly checks at her watch and has to fly like summer birds.

After she is gone an idea dangles at me, like the wave heat from an oven door fast opened. I battle with the frighteners until I am chilled of cold sweat. This idea has a scent to it not the pictures. It is the scent of the back place at Blandish the butchers where I did go to meet with dad. It is the scent of the killing, of lardy flesh and dripping blood on sawdusty floors. I understand from it, that the making open of Pig Palace to Holly means I open pigworld to dreaded dangers. And for some space of time the ground shifts below, as the sea-pulled sand did at the holiday place dad took me one time with the tin bucket and wood spade what carried pictures of sailor boats. But I make realisings that I can not look to time back there, it is done now, the coming in of Holly is as the tumbling tide. It can not be stopped.

In late time pig wanderings I make offerings of tiny mirror pieces at pigrelic stone. This is in proper recognising the power of it to bring connection with Holly and me. I do acknowledgement that dread things could flourish from good and get tremblings within as one cloud immediately blankets the moon from me.

Freya nudges at me to watch her new piggylets at their first water escapade and I take relief from their purest of joy as moon returns to put silver on their backs. It is all of connectedness, moon, water, pigs, hope, Holly, me, all of the cycle round. An owl flies extra low by my head, seeking for mice and birds, her only sound, the shush shushing of furry wings. Life inside death. It goes round, round, round, it never will be still.

EIGHT

Holly Lock's world

When Jack sang for me, throwing his voice out into the corners of his pigdom, it was like the sound a young boy would make in a trained-up choir at some expensive school or cathedral. Sweet and clear as glass. And if I shut my eyes and listened I could imagine the sound came out of someone who looked like an archangel rather than a goblin. When I left him I wanted to go straight round to Colin Driver's house and give him a good kicking for what him and his sick mates had done to Jack. They're pathetic.

Mam was annoyed when I got in because I'd only left myself half an hour to get ready for my birthday party. She had all the sandwiches and cakes set out and was just putting the cream on the trifle.

I apologised but for some reason she wasn't having it, she kept going on at me about why I was late in. It was like doing the party had become a huge chore for her and the weird thing was, it had been her idea to have it. She thought I should be more 'sociable' and maybe she was right, but parties usually made me tongue-tied because I just wasn't very good at all that chitchat.

It wasn't like her to be snappy and short-tempered, though, she usually enjoyed this sort of thing. Yes, she'd tell me off for being late but this was definitely over the top. I remembered the long phone call the night before and her forgetting the bolognese sauce.

When she insisted on knowing where I'd been I lied, saying I was at the skateboard park. She stopped decorating the trifle and stared at me like I was an alien.

'Aren't you ever going to grow up?' she said.

That really hurt. I couldn't understand what was happening or why she was in such a strange mood and I almost told her to forget the party. After telling me to get washed and changed she turned back to the trifle and said, 'And wear something nice for a change.'

By nice, she meant a proper dress or a skirt. At first I thought, no way, on me they looked like they were still on hangers, but upstairs on my own, guilt took over. I was lying to her and secretly seeing Jack Plum. Maybe she could sense something different in me and that's what was making her edgy. As a compromise I tried on a stretchy bra she'd got me which was still in the box. It just sort of hung there like a dodgy hammock. I pushed some tissue paper into the cups to fill them out but when I put a T-shirt on, my breasts looked like two bags of crisps.

The short purple dress she'd bought me for my birthday

turned me into a cross-dresser. I tried walking around in it but my knees seemed to kick out so much they kept catching on the hem. They should give lessons on how to walk in a tight skirt. When I looked at myself in the mirror I felt humiliated. There was no way I was going to the party looking like a transvestite. I flung the dress and the bra into the bottom of my wardrobe.

When I got back downstairs the music was on and Samantha had arrived. That made things worse because I hadn't invited her to the party. She came gushing towards me holding out a small bright-pink box. 'I've bought you some perfume,' she said with a syrupy grin.

'Perfume?' I snorted. 'That's for old ladies.' I didn't want to hurt her but I really didn't like perfume, it always made me sneeze and I must have told her that a dozen times. But then she's never been brilliant in the listening department. She only wanted to be at my party because she'd fallen out with her latest bosom pal, Paula Tompkins. They'd been hanging out together for weeks, linking arms, whispering, mooching off to the chippie at lunchtimes, staying over at each other's houses. Then Paula started seeing this lad who does the mobile buffets on the London to Edinburgh trains and she dumped Samantha. That's why I was flavour of the month, again.

'Don't be pathetic, Holly,' she snapped. 'All the girls in our class wear it, except you. The real girls, I mean. I thought I was doing you a favour.'

That got my back up. Why couldn't she just say sorry for going off with Paula and dumping me? Instead she always just marched back into my life as if she'd never left. 'One,' I snapped, 'I didn't invite you to my party, and two, I don't bloody well like perfume, as you well know.'

'One, your mam invited me, I told her that you said I couldn't come. And two, you should be grateful I'm trying to help you instead of laughing at you the way some of the other girls do.'

I told Samantha she was a creep and walked away. It was supposed to be my bloody party and my list of guests.

Pushing her eyebrows up, Samantha clicked her tongue – like our headmistress, Mrs Wilson, does when she's irritated – and followed me. I just knew she was dying to get some sarcastic comment in. When it came I went hot with shock.

'What were you doing in Pardes Wood yesterday?' she said triumphantly. 'That's where Jack Plum hangs about and you're not supposed to go there.'

I denied being in the woods but she insisted she'd seen me. When she started raising her voice my neck began knotting up with worry. I invited her to stay at the party. And whilst I was rewarded with an ear-to-ear beam job, her eyes stayed sharp and knowing. She does my head in sometimes.

Mam was watching everything from the kitchen doorway. She was obviously unimpressed with my jeans and loose shirt.

I tried to keep out of Samantha's way once the party got going but she was as hard to shift as a sweet paper stuck to your shoe. She cornered me in the corridor between the kitchen and the front room and went on about wanting to be my best friend, again. It wasn't as if I had loads to choose from.

'You always say you're my best friend and then you just bugger off with someone else when you feel like it.'

'Maybe you should try to be a bit more exciting to be with then.' She moved so close I almost couldn't breathe. I was tempted to smack her in the face but mam came up at that moment.

Samantha started smarming up to her as usual, saying what a fab party it was, then she suggested we play games.

'What d'you suggest, Samantha?' mam said, her face had softened a little, which pleased me, but when Samantha suggested Truth, Dare, Kiss or Promise, I groaned loudly.

'No way!' I said. 'I just want music and dancing.'

Mam and Samantha smiled at one another. 'Too grown-up for games, are you?' mam said. My mouth went sour and dry. I wanted to slap mam and Samantha, walk out of the house and into Jack's Pig Palace, but of course I couldn't. Instead I ate too much food and when mam finally gave in to Samantha's endless requests for games, I was so pissed off I raided her drinks cupboard and hid in the pantry swigging Baileys and brandy. I ended up in bed with a whirling head and stomach pains. Laughter and music from downstairs drifted up through the floorboards making me feel more miserable. Some party.

The vomiting started about half an hour later. It was a relief after the horrible tidal wave sensation and I began to feel better almost immediately. But when mam saw me coming down the stairs she sent me straight back up. She said she wanted me to stay in bed. I tried arguing with her but she wouldn't listen, she reckoned my head was too hot. It was as if me being late for the party had set something off in her. But that was stupid, it wasn't a major crime for God's sake.

When she went back downstairs to send everyone home with a bit of cake, I lay there feeling totally irritated. I wondered if there was any way she could have found out about me and Jack but I didn't think so, her reaction would have been much stronger. Then I thought she might know about the brandy and Baileys. I couldn't help groaning out loud, apart from being with Jack it'd been a crap day.

About eight o'clock mam came up with a supper tray. She plumped up my pillows and said she wanted me to stay in bed till morning, in case I'd caught a bug or something. I'd already been cooped up for three hours and I needed to get out of bed. She'd bought me a video as one of my presents and I'd planned to watch it with her. Most of all I wanted to make things right between us. She insisted I stayed in bed.

'What's wrong, mam? Why are you giving me such a hard time?'

She took hold of my hand and gave an embarrassed smile. 'I'm sorry, Holly. You're right, I have been a bit distracted, it's just that, well, I've got something on my mind . . .' She tailed off and I waited for her to finish. 'I've met someone,' she said softly.

My stomach started somersaulting again. She was talking about a boyfriend. It knocked me off balance because I wasn't expecting it. I stared at her and realised she was a bit more dressed up than usual.

'You mean you've got a date?' She nodded and brushed my hair back off my face. 'Tonight?'

'Is that a problem?' she asked.

Of course it was a problem. I didn't want her to have a boyfriend because it meant I'd see less of her and he'd be coming to our house.

'Does it have to be tonight? Only I wanted us to be together, y'know, after my party.'

'I thought you wouldn't mind me going out for a while after I'd done such a nice party for you. I didn't expect you to get sick, sweetheart . . . it's all arranged and I've been looking forward to it . . . you don't really mind, do you?'

I did and I suppose I could have got all miserable on her but then we wouldn't have had a good time together anyway.

'I could get Samantha to come and stay with you, have a stopover.'

I wasn't in the mood for Samantha, in fact I wasn't in the

mood for anything much, so I just shook my head. She leant closer and stroked my forehead, which really was hot by then.

'Things change, Holly,' she said softly.

I stayed in bed while she finished getting ready. Part of me thought she might still change her mind, come back into my room wearing her jogging pants and a T-shirt and put her arms around me. So when I heard the taxi horn outside, and her footsteps on the path, I was dismal.

Watching the video on my own didn't seem a very attractive option, so I tumbled out of bed, got washed and changed and pinned a note on my door which said:

DO NOT DISTURB

After checking my plants I barricaded my bedroom door from the inside, checked no one was watching and climbed on to my window ledge. My bedroom's above the garage. The main window looks out on to the street but the other one's over the side of the garage. There's this high metal gate below some old trellising, which used to have ivy all over it, until dad poisoned it. It's possible to climb off my window ledge, down the trellising and on to the gate without much difficulty. Jack would be pleased to see me and I didn't see why I should be on my own on my party night.

NINE

All about pigs

Mam's bloodcoughing came full halt up on a week of time and made good feelings in both her and me, even though it is not to be talked about between a mam who doesn't want to be a mam and a ugly disappointing son. Holly Lock tries to visit with me and the pigs every day. She even came especial on her birth day night to cuddle at Peach and talk of some disappointments on account her mam had gone to other entertainments. Some times she can stay only for small minutes but others for more than one hour. She causes hope within my spaces and cheerfulness and fills up the empty place dad's leaving made. And I splat away any frighteners what creep up on me about bad invasions from the outsideworld. She is full up with questions at all times, she wants to know all I can tell about pigs.

'They can do . . . anything,' I say and she always wants grasp on the details of it. 'They can dance . . . pull a cart, scent out . . . landmines, walk . . . at heel . . . learn their toilet training . . . faster than dogs . . . play xylophone . . .'

'Yeah,' she says, 'I wanted to know about the toilet stuff. Where do they do it, because it doesn't smell like pig muck in here?'

I show her the chemically place I made, up by the outsidepigdoor, and she is full amazed at the cleverness of it and I get perky with my pride.

'You mean you can toilet train them, just like a toddler?'

'Humanpigs train the canines and felines, and pigs is cleverer so is easy.'

'Wow,' she says. 'Cool.' She has a big liking for things to be 'cool', which means 'extreme good' to her. More space spent in with Holly gives me new words and ways of saying, so it is 'cool'. And she takes all of the learning I give, up into that brain space, sucks at it like the hoover cleaner and recalls all I tell. Her mind apparatus is extreme good and I am in pleasure of that. What ever happens at my life Holly will have full potential of success in all she does choose, this I know.

But she says on about not believing the truth of the xylophone thing until Freya shows it, plonkity plonking with her trotters at the coloured metals of the xylophone toy, ears twitching this way that and making a choppy tune what me nor Holly have ever heard the like of. And Holly's laughing fills up the whole of the Palace, as sweet roses does.

Some times Holly sits and reads in the *Pig Breeder* magazines what dad left and she says out bits of things to me.

Some which I do know, some I do not.

'Look, Jack, it says pigs quickly learn how to use automatic feeding systems and can operate a flush water system to clean out their pens.'

'Yes, I telled that. Very clever pigs . . . very clean.'

And she tells me on pigs and myths . . . of Hercules – who she names one of the strongest men of the outside-world long time past – that he did wrestle a large boar called Erymanthian for one of twelve trials he got given. I would not wrestle Freya, I tell.

'No, neither would I. Look at her, Jack, she's smiling, look!'

I say how she knows of the name. 'Freya! Freya! Freya!' I speak it extreme loud and Freya stomps and snorts and splashes water up high by plopping her fat body in to the pool. Holly gets pain in her side from the laughing, which she calls 'stitching' and she falls from her hay bale like skittles at the fair ground Hoppings. Topple. When her ribs get better from the crunch of the fall she gets the serious face on.

'I want everyone to know how clever you are, Jack Plum. It's not fair how they think of you as just this ugly Freak.'

'Is what you thought, Holly.'

'I know and you do look scary but now I know you're not and I want them all to understand how clever and kind you are.'

I shake my hoghead extreme fast because I get the quick

frightener rush, up from the toes all up into the head and it judders, clang, clang. It is like a premonition thing, dad said one time I was extreme good at this, knowing what might wait up ahead, and I must make Holly not speak, not tell anything of the Palace to the outsidepeople.

'Want is not just enough, Holly,' I say. 'Want can not stop runaway trains, or hurricanes, or changes, like the catching of the wind can not be done. This is secret, Holly, that was the promise you did make.'

She turns off from me to play with Peach, and hums a jumpy tune. She does this for some minutes and I make busy with cleaning old hay to the outer door and pulling new bales from the high stack I builded last autumn time. In some while she goes at my cupboard.

'Question time again, Jack,' she says, and I know all is as was. She loves the questioning of me and what I have in memory and it works good for my special knowing.

'Right, here goes. "The work of teaching and organising the others fell naturally to the pigs, who were generally recognised as being the cleverest of the animals." Come on, Jack, you know this one.'

'*Animal Farm*.'

'Excellent.'

'We liked . . . old Major pig . . . best.'

'I bet you did. Now, try this one, and keep your eyes closed, no cheating.'

The pigs begin to squeal and scud about for they pick up

excitement of the quizzing and my outsidepeople frighten-er disappears out through my skin leaving just coldness at the edges.

She set the little creature down, and felt quite relieved to see it trot quietly into the wood. 'If it had grown up,' she said to herself, 'it would have made a dreadfully ugly child; but it makes a rather handsome pig, I think.'

I have chances here to show I am more than my body tells and there is joy fullness to the pleasing of Holly with proper answers so I name *Alice in Wonderland*.

'Yes, yes, yes. Brilliant, Jack.'

She stops reading and stares bright on me and I feel awk-ward in my bigness. She wants knowledge of my miss shape, the how and why of it, so I tell what was made known to me. That the big head makes the brain machine slow to give thoughts to my mouth. Then she does question on schoolthings in past time and I make explanation how I stayed with mam . . . for help . . . and how she got lonely . . . after dad and did want me close at her all times.

'But how d'you know your brain's slow if you didn't go to school?'

I tell what mam said of my empty hoghead what does not take in proper knowing.

'You're kidding me, Jack Plum. How could you build all of this if you were brainless, eh? How could you? I couldn't do it and I've been going to school for years and years. And what about all the book questions I ask you? Knowing all that needs a proper brain.'

I believe she has intent to pride me up with these words and that is good, her not wanting the notice of my damage. And her questions come on and on like water does fall.

'How old are you, Jack? D'you know?'

I explain how I do not know the full years but it is some thing like ten and ten and ten and some extra.

'Mid-thirties then – hey, you're nearly old enough to be my dad! That's weird.' And she goes right within her thought spaces and her eyes do look off sideways for some little while.

'D'you believe in God, Jack?' she does say then.

My thoughts is taken in surprise at this. 'That is one big question, not a pig question,' I tell and this gives her much laughing.

'You're a poet, Jack,' she says, '"a big question, not a pig question" – but what about God, do you think about that? We're doing stuff at school about it, different religions from round the world and I think it's really confusing. D'you think there's a God up there?'

She makes a finger to the sky. These things I have done some thoughts on. Mam has God beliefs but dad had soul thoughts. He told of many souls, maybe a full million, what got rebirthed over and over. He said they was of total energy, like a titchy bit of the sun. That is to explain when humanpigs have the skull memory of times past. There is a core text – within the brain space – what has all remembrance of all things. Dad told that if we could know the access of it, the world insideout is explained. I give all this telling to Holly and she swirls it about much for a time before the questioning erupts.

'So you think that when babies are born, they bring all that knowledge with them, but hidden in a special part of the brain? Is that it?'

I tell it is some thing of the like and how dad told that babies do choose their arriving, meaning that I made selection of the turf and turmoil of my place.

'That seems weird, Jack, do you believe it?'

I tell her I have no sureness, though I see the core text place I think, when I go inside. It is close at the memories-gone shelf, in the forefront brain. Holly does not take in this stuff with ease but she smiles radiant anyways.

'Y'know what?' she says. 'I really like it here, Jack. No teachers. No parents. No Samantha. No one telling us what we can and can't do. No one forcing us to grow up.'

'And piggies.'

'And piggies, of course. Jack . . . y'know that pig stone you told me about, the one you make wishes on?'

'Pigrelicstone.'

'Could I make a wish for my school to burn down so I don't have to go for a while?'

I give explanation how you must not spoil the wishing thing for making badness.

'I don't want anyone to get hurt, just the building to go.'

But I do insist it is not the pigrelicstone way and then she does have to leave. I stand in full stillness until the scent and warm of her is gone and gets the feel of an emptiness coming open, as a hole could, what she did brim up with joyfulness. Now it will stay unfilled, a remembrance of her until she does return with her outsideness and all her prospects for a big, open life and a future of fulfillness and plans.

Mam is in the sleep of the whisky when I go upsteps. I gather her to my arms and carry her for the bed and she feels extreme light, more lightness than I do ever remember. She begins a singing with the stairs climb, *Black is the Colour of my True Love's Hair*, one of her favouritest. I trunch her up on the bed and she presses her face next to my bristling skin and slurps out words what ask if I do love her still, which she has not for some long time.

I tell that I do and the feel of her lovingness slipping towards me does heat my body full to the hoghead. She makes blame for the oftentimes mean words she lashes at me up on the pains within. This I can make understanding of but I gets a sad throat when she puts all the fault of it up on dad and his leaving. To comfort her, I make soothe noises and stroke up on her hand and do tuck bedclothes to her neck and pat down the sides to keep draughty things out, as dad did always for me.

But as I make for leaving she grips at my clothes and asks

me to linger on and sing her into dreamland. I get pleasure to do this for her, but first, I make a grasp on this softness moment to question the reasons for the hoghead.

Firstly she does not make understanding of my words, but slow it comes slurping out from her that the doctors, what she hates, made use of equipment, named forceps, to twist and drag me from inside of her, to the outside world. And she has insistence that they are the blame for the baby Jack head damage. But when I make more questions she tells that my brains was not much hurt, only the head casing. This is unknown to me beforetimes.

Then she is too far towards sleeptime to give talk and I gets a dredged up longing for her to come soft all ways, to give up love at me in place of the anger, to help me make the better words for her. But in my soul heart I knows it will not be so.

I sing *Catch the Wind* because I have the liking for it, but inside of me the thought comes up strong, my head is not empty, and she telled that it was, for all those years long. Why did she not send me for the school to put learning in? Was it on account of the ugliness? And I churn up in my belly like curdling milk, with the thoughts of, what if. Thoughts what have never come to visit my hog skull before. When mam snores sleep around the walls, my head cavern stomps as a pig's rampage and I know I will get no comfort in dream time.

I turn myself away from her to go to the company of my

pigs and she begins a choking up. She pushes up, right from flat down and the cough comes hurtling as a bucking boar and blood spurtles over the creamy bedcover, like it has been storing itself.

The bloodcoughing goes on into all the night. I change bedcoverings two times, until there is none left and I get the wash machine to work on the blood and gobby stuff mam heaves out. My own stomach bubbles with the stink of it all and piggies do not get their outsidetime in Pardes Wood till almost the sun-up. It is the worst in-the-wood time we ever have made, as I am wretched with thoughts of mam and blood, and the pigs are wretched up in sympathy of me.

I tumble in sleep for some time before a thwumping sound rips me awake. Mam has slid downsteps, nearly to the end, and lies in heaps. I believe she was on the whisky hunt but I hump her on shoulder tops back to her bed for more resting.

At the bed she makes shaky points at her bottles of medicines. There is fear, full within her, and I see that we have some near empties of pills. Being attended on Holly I have forgot this routine. This day I must make the visit at the doctor place for repeating of pill sheet. I do not like the desk woman there, pinching her lips at me, all ways.

Later time I give mam soup and bread but she is not wanting it, only whisky and sleep. I give one only whisky measure for I have fear of the choking.

I get clear the streets without kiddypig ambushing but within the doctors is lots of them and adult humanpigs waiting. The desk woman does some little shudder as I put mam's note at her. It is grubby from much using and from my pocket depths but mam was not waked up to do new versions.

The woman does the lip pinch as predicted as I wait in silence for the time I must fetch new pill sheet. But she does go at her machine and press on many buttons and I do just stand. I can not leave until pill sheet collection time is got. I see her make a small look like pleasure as she comes at me again.

'The doctor needs to examine your mother before we can issue another repeat prescription,' she says in extreme slowness and extra loud as she was talking to a baby. This is greatly serious. I had forgot of his visits this every often-time.

'Thursday morning, after surgery,' she says, and I do rock foot to foot in worry and confused. She does a snort as an old sow and points off the days on her chart, one, two, three days on. I am out that room and at the street speedily for my hoghead does wallop.

When Holly Lock calls at her trekking from the school I am become as a slobber face with fear of doctor and the outsideworld coming in on me and seeing mam in the bloodcoughing way. If she does get to hospital I might get to being locked away as mam has said often.

'What is it, Jack? Don't cry, please, look how upset the pigs are. Tell me what's wrong, maybe I can help.'

I see the frighteners close at Holly and fear up on her eyes, not of me but for me. Since dad I have no body to give words and things to, except the pigs, and the closeness of Holly unblocks inmost terrors in me and I blurt out at her, all my big worry things about being locked up in the outsideworld if mam leaves, or is shunted to hospital . . . or dies.

I tell on how the doctor must come, Thursday, for repeating prescriptions and how mam says they'll take me away because I did not care after her proper.

'Your mam's just being nasty, Jack, she's trying to scare you, to make you keep doing what she wants.'

'But they do come.'

'It's only Monday, Jack, we've got time to sort something out. Don't let your mam get at you.'

Then I give out my worries on mam making big coughs and some blood stuff again. How it is not good stuff for me or doctor to see.

'Listen, Jack, I promise I'll find a way to save you and the pigs. If people knew how clever you are, if they could see what you've built down here . . .'

These words of outsideworld humanpigs do make my voice come out big in frights. I tell an other time, how it can not be, how they have hate of me and I do stamp of my feet to make notice of the importance. This does make some small shocks within her, to hear the deepest of my hogvoice but she does take breaths and steps back and does accept.

'Okay, Jack . . . it's okay. I won't let you down. Listen, how often does the doctor come and check up on your mam? Can you remember?'

And we do go into the pattern of the thing, to look for solution. I give answers to all the needed questions, like how the doctor does make visits to mam round each half year. I know of this, on account I made check up on my Blandish the butcher calendar. And how it is Doctor Taylor at Derwent Street what comes to do prescribing.

'Great, because he doesn't know me, we go to the Richmond Road practice. I'll make a plan, don't worry, we'll sort it out.'

She has such sureness on her and being within her certainness makes me get stronger. If there is a way she will uncover it and the Palace will be saved. She stays an extra long time and I have worry that her mam will start the ringing bells of fear thing.

'Don't worry about her,' Holly says. 'She's got other things on her mind at the moment.'

'Then you might come for our outside time?' I say. 'Have the ride on Freya?'

She jumps up with excitedness and joy and leap dances all around and the pigs get infected of her. After the big rumpus is calmed some, I tell Holly of the longness of pig riding with humanpigs. It was told in a book of dad's that it began in the islands of Indo Nesia, when a learning monk had a journey there. It was a testing thing for him, a trial, and he was in pain of his legs. For him to not give it up he rested long aside a tribe of Babyrussa grey pigs, which in a picture look as small elephant types with no trunks. They darted off from him firstly when he was mingling, but his monk stillness made them not fearful and even the big tusky ones came near. And this monk rode one pig, named Quinling, to the appointed test place and his legs was preserved. This Quinling tusker then stayed tribing with him for all of twenty years gone.

Holly likes this knowing extreme much and it comes to outsideriding Freya and she is easy for it, gentle and whispering, as it should be with pigs, and Peach is there always, running, and snorting on behind them. And Holly cannot stop her words of wonder at pigriding as I suspected. But then she does stop and splat to ground for staring and she calls at me to see.

'It's called the greater butterfly orchid, Jack, isn't it beautiful? Look, the flowers are like a butterfly, aren't they?'

This is true, it is as a white butterfly up on the grassy green stalks.

'And smell it, Jack, it's vanilla, isn't it gorgeous?'

I never did sniff at something so sweet and am full amazed at Holly's knowing all of this, which I tell and she does explain her loving of plants and how they are all so differing and full of interest. In future times she does want to make her outsideworld in looking after them, breeding them up, as I do my pigs and maybe naming them, also as I do with my pigs. With eyes full sparkling she gives me especial naming of this butterfly plant. It is made in an other language which is Latin and is called *Platanthera chlorantha*. The words does lollop and roll up on my tongue. It is as music, up and down. I have no knowledges of other language speaking, it is a new thought. And when I do tell Holly, she gives news of all differing speakings in the huge farlands world.

Many leaves fly off from trees this nighttime, and I make runs at them to catch but they was too darty and driven by mischief wind. To catch the leaf on first fall is extreme fortune. The woods have the strong scents of wild garlic slivered with honeysuckle which Freya brings back within the Palace after many chomps. It beds on the air for some hours in reminder of outside time.

When Holly leaves I think more on her words. It has been promised she will give help and I feel better with that in my hoghead. Mam is far off asleep when I go to there. Her chest area is shudders and croaks and there is one long spittle of the brightest blood what leaks from one corner of the mouth, down way past her ear.

My dreamworld is full brimming of red flowers and garlic smells and vanilla, and there is distance noises what comes nearer in a regular time, as a drum beat would and when I gasp awake in dreadful fear and sweating I understand the drum is my hammerful heart pumped on about worries and frighteners waiting on the edges of things. All times they seek for inspaces. The worry stuff and the fear fulls is what lets them full into brain space. Got inside they do rattle and venom and devour up strongness and joy fullness.

TEN

Holly Lock's world

When I got to bed I tried to recall every little detail of riding on Freya. The warm, itchy feel of her back between my legs; the gentle rocking movement as she swayed from side to side when she walked. It was like I was in a trance. Jack showed me how to steer with my knees and how to whisper words of encouragement into those big flappy ears that were never still for one moment. And when Freya ran I could almost feel what it might be like to fly. I've dreamt about flying and I'm always running towards a cliff top, taking off then swooping down towards tiny people on a sandy beach. Being on Freya's back gave me the same whooshing feeling, like the best roller coaster ride.

Mam didn't get home till late again last night so it must have been another date. When I got in my tea was in the fridge, with a note on the table about heating it up. It was a nice note and there was special pecan ice cream as a treat but I really missed having her around to chat with. The house seemed deserted without her singing and messing about. It's partly my fault, not coming straight home from school, but I like to be there to feed Peach myself when I can. The problem is that I can't explain and so she probably thinks I'm deliberately avoiding her.

I was lying down, thinking about Jack and the pigs, when I heard her on the stairs. She knocked on my door, came straight in and switched on my bedroom light. She's not supposed to do that, we have a deal. It's my room and I have to invite people in.

She sat on my bed and started talking really fast and I realised she was a bit drunk. It was quite funny in a way because I hadn't seen her tipsy since Christmas. The smell of cigarettes wasn't very nice, though, and that was new. I turned my head away from the sour smell and she must have thought I was sulking. She kept going on about how we needed to sort things out.

When I didn't reply her voice got slightly sharper and she started saying how she hadn't planned to meet someone so special; how she didn't want it to cause problems between me and her; how she knew she hadn't handled it well. I turned back to her and told her it was all right, but truthfully I hoped that the dates wouldn't last, that either he'd get fed up or she would, then everything would get back to normal. Meanwhile I thought it best to say as little as possible.

Then she really floored me by doing this stupid giggle and saying I'd understand everything soon because I'd be going out on dates myself. Why did she have to say that, when she knew it wasn't true? Maybe it was wishful thinking, on her part, not mine.

Once I was alone I started thinking about it. She really should've warned me she'd met someone, got me used to the idea before she started dating seriously. I knew men sometimes went a bit crazy when they fell for someone. Now I couldn't help wondering if women ran off with new guys and left their kids behind.

Everything was so easy in the Palace with Jack and the pigs. No pressures, no arguments, no Samantha and no boyfriends getting in the way. It was like some sort of fate, me getting to know him just when mam starting dating this guy. Thinking of fate reminded me of the tarot, which mam seemed to have abandoned, now that her life was so full of other, better things. I crept downstairs, got the pack out of the drawer in the living room, laid it out on my floor the way mam always did and closed my eyes. I asked if it was fate that I'd met Jack. My finger was resting right in the middle of one particular card when I opened my eyes a few seconds later.

It was 'The Fool'. This is a figure on a journey, walking towards the edge of a cliff, holding a flower in his hand. I knew it was a card about risk but that was all, so I read the interpretation in the book which mam kept with the pack:

> *The Fool represents the innocent person who takes a leap of faith to gain wisdom and insight. S/he steps*

forth without regard to warning and is free to make choices. S/he knows there will be consequences but also knows that risks must be taken in order to gain experience and mature. The card does NOT mean that you are a fool but perhaps you are trying to avoid the more difficult aspects of a particular situation. Becoming mature means facing up to the positive and negative forces in life.

I took that as a 'yes'. It was fate meeting Jack. Mam was off doing her own thing and instead of getting fed up I'd got him. Jack and the pigs were like my new family, I was part of their tribe and had to stop thinking about the way things used to be and plan for the future. Easier said than done. But if I had to make a plan, it would be for me and Jack to find a wild farm somewhere, with lots of space for the pigs and for me to grow plants and trees. There'd be a huge greenhouse and a conservatory and Jack would never have to hide from people again. It sounded more like a wish than a plan.

ELEVEN

Mrs Plum

Mam gets into her early self for some of the deep of dark morning time. She calls out at me as if I am the hogboyJack again. She is in memory of the visit we made to the place of York, me, her and dad. It was brim full of huge trains what did not move but rested up for all to see. Some was as big as houses in colours of forest green, rosehip red and gold. In her memory time mam sees the pigboy and says out sweet words at me and strokes on my hair and arms as she had forgot me as gargoyle.

I ask then about dad and about the love between them. I like to hear good words on dad.

'He was the handsomest man around these parts, Jack. I saw him at the Summer Ball in the Assembly Rooms in Newcastle and I made sure he danced with me.' She laughed from some long place back before the bitterness times came into her, a laugh for my young dad. 'He was just like a film star, Jack, and he chose me . . . me.' Then the bloodcoughing stuff came on and all memories was abandoned to the bile and puke and spew and as I cleaned and wiped I got full of thoughts on the misplaced things what we have stored within the skull.

A time later Holly comes and plays her flute with us and I have understanding that her comings to the Palace is now sanctuary for her as well as me and the pigs. We is tribe, bonding together. She has sadness up on her and tells it is of worries up on her mam. She is brimmed up in her thoughts but the music playing and the pig prancing soon puts all into much more calmness. She tells then how she has been thinking on plans to do with the doctor visit and other times to come. She wants to know of lots of things: like persons what come to the house and the how often and the how I get money stuff and if I can make mam's voice like I throw around my own, which I can, so I show her.

'"Jack . . . Jack . . . fetch me some tea, at once!"' I go.

'That's excellent, Jack!' Holly says. 'That's what we need. And you say nobody comes to the house, except sometimes selling things and the doctor every six months or so and you fetch the prescriptions, right?'

I get mam's money book for Holly to see and she does writing within her flute book. 'Look, Jack,' she says some while on, 'I'm really good at copying things and I've been trying out your mam's signature off the pension book, see.'

And there it lays, one clean page, and mam's lollopy name as if marked by her.

'I'll be able to sign the pension book every week, so even

if something does happen to your mam, you'll be okay, you'll have money for food and things.'

I tell how very clever she is with the signing and thinking on future things.

'We'll sort it out, Jack, you and me,' Holly says. 'I'll be here, I'll help you, I won't let them take you away. We just have to keep you safe until I'm a bit older, then I can make sure you and the pigs are all right and mam can go off with whoever she wants.'

I tell her she is full of kind stuff but at my inner deepness I know there is not one probable of longtime future things for me and Holly. There is just this momentness, this now time.

'Now on Thursday,' she says, 'we have to make sure your mam has quite a bit of whisky before the doctor comes, okay?'

'So she is not sensible?'

'Exactly. The doctor will smell the whisky anyway so he won't expect too much sense. I'll be here when he comes and I'll say I'm your cousin. I'll tell him that my mam pops in to make sure your mam is okay and she sends me over with food and stuff.'

'And doctor will get assurance of things being proper and well.'

'Yes, and if he should say anything about you, I'll tell him you'll be coming to live with us if anything happens to your mam. See?'

She does beam on account of her bright ideas and I say she gets cleverer than a pig.

'I'll take that as a compliment, Jack,' she says, with much laughs, and I sees her heart is less of heaviness than on her coming.

We are all much quiet for some while, it is rest and think time. Only the piggylets make noise, snaffling at Freya for milkings. I try and think on about other things than blood and my head dwells up on dad and if he could get found. I do not think on those ideas of usual because they make for unsettlement but blood thoughts is even worse, not knowing the happening of things is worse still. I ask Holly will she come to observe at mam.

'We'll have to be very careful. What if she wakes up and sees me? She might scream or something and bring the neighbours running,' Holly says.

I do make reminder that neighbours never come into here and have no notice of noise but that Samantha did come by the end garden past daytime, like she was seeking and I make strong words on keeping the Palace secret from the outsideworld.

'Honestly, I wouldn't tell anyone, especially not Samantha, she's just a nosy sod. She's always following me around. I promised, Jack, and I never break my promises.'

I tell that I also never would break of a promise and she stares at me long times with no words.

'Will you make a promise to me, Jack?' she says then.

I ask of what.

'Will you promise never to leave me and go off with someone else like mam has?' And she does look earth space, like she has worries that I will not promise.

'I do promise on my deep soul heart and on sweet inmemories of dad, that I will never leave you as long as I do live.' I hold out my hog hand to her titchy and when she does splat I see tears within her eyes. That does make my hog heartspace full of ache for her and when she does lean her head in to my hog chest I do not move off from her as is usual. I do let her take the warm from me as long as is her needfulness.

When she is in strength again we toetip the cellar upsteps with cotton wool feet as the pigs murmur softly beneath. At the top I open the door midwide to wait. Nothing sounds but the ticktocking wooden clock, what throws my head back into childspace when dad showed how to know time. Holly follows close up on the hall and carpet steps. I hear her breathe all raggedy, as she is holding it and forgetting to let more in.

We stop at the outside mam's door, which does its awkward creak at the push open. The whisky smell is in there, sharp on the inside nose and I must squeeze at my nostrils to stop getting sneezy. Mam faces out at us, her chin berry-red of streaky blood. Holly's body makes a jerk and when I look she is still as rabbits in torchlight. But at my move close by the bed she moves also, step up on step.

We still have some space off when mam makes the sudden lurch fast forward, forced up with the cough urge and more blood does expel and dribble from the mouth. Holly makes a cry out for the horrible sight of it and stumbles for the door space to hold. I did forget the gore of it and now see it in Holly's eyes. Mam tries to make my name and it gets lost within the gurgling throat as she lumbers back at her pillows.

Holly's face is full drained with fright. When I do touch her titch hand she makes a jump and a gasping.

'She looks dreadful,' Holly does whisper. 'All that blood and stuff. What is it? Why is she coughing all that up?'

Holly does stumble more, far back at the wall and slithers it to the floor. There is a canine panting in her and I wonder if vomits will come. I go to fetch new water for her but she does grab up on my leg.

'Don't leave me here on my own, please,' she whispers. So I do help her to the downsteps and water which she does drink up quick.

'How can you stand it, Jack? It's so awful, the smell and everything.'

'I do clean her regular, change sheets and clothes . . .'

'Oh Jack, I didn't realise, you poor thing.'

'Not poor, Holly, it is what must get done.'

'Have you got any idea what's wrong with her?'

'Dad all ways telled it was the Deep pression what made her sickness.'

'I don't know about all that, Jack. I'm sorry, but I don't think it's depression that's making her cough up the blood and everything.'

I fill up more new water for mam and I do tell Holly that the bloodcoughing did come on mam earlier times and did then go off again and so it may be this time. I say she can go back to the Palace but she makes a shake of her head and does some gulping and catches hold on my jacket. We go extreme slow and quiet on the upsteps and stands close in on the bed, looking on mam in quiet, and is both fully jolted when she snaps her lids to full open. Her eyes is streaked of blood and full up of spite as she does glare on Holly. And I do make notice of the awfulness of it all as not before. The blood up on her face and clothes, the vomit in clumps on pillow and sheet, tissues grimed with muck and spittle all over everywhere.

Holly does have one hand pressed up on her mouth and one grasping tight my jacket as mam opens her mouth to screech.

Holly lets drop my jacket and moves some steps off at mam's words and does try to pull me away also. I try my own speech to make answer to mam but it does come out as full garble and Holly takes the place and makes to speech with mam when the bloodcoughing grabs at her hard and Holly does run off to the downsteps with little whimpers.

When mam has spilled more and more blood and slime

on to the covers she does fall back deep into pillows with dark blood splutterings foaming at her chin. My inside nub wants to rage up on her and blast her disgusting mouth for this ugly spite on Holly, but she goes quick into deep rasps of breathing without conscience of me, and my fury does dribble off. The big frightener what I had before times wants in at me, telling that outsidepeople will come after the doctor does and they will curse of me and send to locking up places where I will have no pigs and no Holly. The raging comes up in me again, wanting me to take all mam's breath from her, to press pillows on to her bloody face and finish life total. My hands does even reach at her scraggy throat but I fight the rage and close my mind to my inspaces and block all the horror with thoughts of piglove.

Within the Palace Holly waits, full surrounded by pig attentions. She is feared of mam now, feared of the sight and stench and disgustful words. Peach does snuggle at her neck making small snory sounds and Holly does stroke at her but her eyes is faraway off on thoughts of blood and stink before she does say more.

'Listen, Jack, we can't let your mam see the doctor, even if she's tipsy, she could say something about me or you that might set him off. It's too risky.'

I is feared because he does come one day, two days on, and my hogvoice comes out harsh and loud in my struggling with the frighteners when I do say this and Holly does get more fear fulls within her eyes until I tell sorry.

'It's all right, Jack. I'll work it out tonight when my head's a bit steadier. I'll find a way to deal with it, I promise.'

We sit on in stillness up on the hay, both of us in full shakiness. Freya does finish up the feeding of piggylets and she makes the lean in against me, swaying as she was listening at music from some long way off. It makes a comfort, this leaning and swaying and soon we all get at it and I hum little snatches of *Catch the Wind* for the settle of us.

'Why do dads go off like that, Jack? D'you know?' Holly asks in her hush hush voice, like it is the question much asked before times, insideout her head. I think the badness of mam, her disease, and also her horrible screeching does shake Holly's courage.

'Many . . . of reasons . . . maybe.'

'Mam says my dad ran off with a petrol pump attendant . . . that's what they do, isn't it, run off with other women, or sometimes other men, like Colin Driver's dad did. They were all talking about that for weeks.'

'Boys get restless in all regions and make up to restless men, if they could make piggylets it could fetch more calm, maybe.'

'You mean make babies?'

'Yes, can not make babies of themselves and this makes them twisty, but I have baby piggylets and some of them men have the canines, and the horses, the footballs, the cars, the motorbikes, lots of . . . stuff in the stead of piggylets.'

'Kids get in the way, that's the problem. Like my mam with this bloke, she seems to want to be with him more and more.'

I have no cheer up words for this, it is not in my knowledge, so I do keep the silence.

Peach comes snuggling back and Holly picks up and does topsnout kissing and hugs and after some while she does look to me.

'I did some research, Jack, on the internet, about your big head and your big body,' she says.

I do not know internet so she does make explaining, it is extreme massive knowledge box what works from electrics and radio and phone things what you can ask great questions from.

'They call it macro . . . cephaly if you've got an abnormal head size. It can be caused by lots of different things. There was this skull in a museum in France, which is a country across the sea, and it belonged to a guy who'd died hundreds of years ago. He was only four feet tall – that's even smaller than me – but his head was three foot round and one foot high. And there was one man who had to have a cushion fixed on each of his shoulders to prop his huge head up and there was another one who couldn't ever lie down because his head was so big.'

'So my hoghead is not so extreme of trouble.'

'No, it's not. But most important, these men were all very

intelligent, Jack. A big head doesn't mean a useless brain, see?'

I ask can the head be made littler.

'I don't think so, Jack – depends on what caused it. Could be genetic, that's something passed on in your family; or caused by a virus and then there's something called Proteus Syndrome . . .'

I make explanation on what mam said on forceps what did damage at my birthing, like if piggylet has to get forced out because they is stuck within sow.

'It might be that, but whatever, you are not brainless, you are a clever pigman.'

'As dad.'

'Yeah . . . like your dad.'

I fill on pride with this but notice of more questionings behind Holly's eyes.

'If we could find out where your dad went, he might come back now your mam's really ill. What d'you think?'

Her words do fill me of longing and the ache of his being gone from me pushes at my chest like cement within a dropped sack. It will all ways be in my front memory space, him there at breakfasting time, then never again. Holly does guess of me deep in despairs on this and offers some solutioning.

'Maybe there's some papers, documents, letters . . . something. Does your mam have a special box where she keeps things? My mam's got a little blue suitcase with birth certificates, photos, bits and pieces. Mementoes she calls them . . . keepsakes, souvenirs.'

I think my head up on this, I make the past pictures of mam at something other than whisky drinks and TV stuff, way back when, and then I see it.

'ScrapBook?' I say.

'Yes, that's the sort of thing. Where does she keep it?'

'Not seen . . . for some long time.'

My inmind stays still back on that picture of mam as she strokes the photos in ScrapBook. She had this red top pot what had a brush in . . . a glue pot, that is the name, and she stuck things on to apricot pages. That was before I came eight years, before dad went, even before the bad whisky days.

'I have to go now and you must start searching tonight, Jack, it could be important.'

I make nods.

'Will you be okay, cleaning up all that mess?'

I tell that I will think my brain away to other things and then I can do.

'When I come tomorrow I'll have a solution to the doctor situation, that's my promise.'

I know Holly is in the right. I must make to find things out, make the plans, and she will help with the carrying out of what has to be done. And I allow a hope to creep into me, a wish of finding dad and with that to know of his leaving, the why and the where. Partly though I get worrisome as it is a might or maybe, not a definite. I busy myself in downsteps drawers, making a seek through life clutter what mam has placed there, batteries, old smelly purses, glistering jewellery what is broke, pencils, and stuff I have no names of, but not ScrapBook.

In deep darktime, beyond pig nighttimetrotting, mam is still in deep snoring land. I have made much cleaning and do feel sick and disgust at the stench of it all and I go street collecting to fetch my brain and my nose off from blood. There is whiskertoms about and one hedgeyhog and night-time birds so I am not the only one to splodge within shad-owtime. I do pause next Samantha's house and deep inside her walls I hear of strange crack sounds as the bricks and cement did hear much they could not hold in. And soon after there comes full hollow stillness all around until four counts and, with great flashing, hailstones do crunch down at roads and roofs. They are big as snowberries and ratch at my face real gristly and I do make inside hopes of them not being some signal of more danger times to come.

TWELVE

Holly Lock's world

Mam was watching TV when I got back and I was glad not to be on my own. The image of Mrs Plum in that bed, surrounded by all that bloody mess, kept flashing back at me. Her horrible voice rang inside my head and I just knew how much pain Jack had put up with from her over the years. I had a shower and put on crisp, clean pyjamas before going downstairs. There was no way I could get to sleep straight away, I had to find something else to focus on. I sat on the small sofa across from mam. She was watching some gardening makeover show. I wanted her to notice I was a bit upset and put her arms round me and make everything feel safe again.

'Finished your homework?' she asked.

I nodded and continued watching her. I could tell she wasn't really interested in the programme. It's me that's always been interested in plants but not these rockery things. Just as they switched to foxgloves, *digitalis purpurea*, which I am interested in, she turned the TV off with the remote and patted the sofa she was on, encouraging me to sit next to her.

I smiled back but stayed where I was. For all I knew Romeo might turn up at any minute.

'No date tonight?' I said.

'No, I wanted to be here with you. I know you're feeling a bit left out and I know it's my fault.'

Seemed like a good time to talk. 'How long have you been seeing him?'

'About six months.'

'And you only told me the night of my party, and only then because I didn't want you to go out?' My throat filled with feathers. I was surprised just how choked up I was.

'I should have told you earlier but I was waiting to see how it went. I mean, if it turned out not to be serious, there was no point in worrying you, was there?'

'So you've had other dates without me knowing?'

'Of course I have.'

This was news to me. I suppose I'd assumed she was working late or out with friends. It felt weird, thinking of her going out with different men. Something must have shown on my face.

'It's perfectly natural.'

'So how many different "dates" have you had since dad left?'

She bit her lip and screwed up her eyes like she was thinking hard. My neck started to get hot.

'Three or four – not exactly Mae West.'

'Who?'

'Just a joke. You look so serious. She was a film star who got through a lot of men.'

'So this one's number five then?'

'His name's Antony.'

'Right.'

She got up and went into the kitchen and I heard her fill the kettle. Then she put her head round the door and asked if I wanted some toast. I told her I wasn't hungry. The sight of Mrs Plum had put me right off food.

'By the way,' she said then, changing the tone of her voice, 'why did you leave so early this morning?'

'Music practice.'

'Samantha said you were late for school.'

'She tells lies. She's a right sad bitch.'

'Holly!'

'I was in the music room,' I lied.

'She said she looked there.'

Mam's lie-catcher eyes turned on me.

'When she's not dumping me for some other girl, she follows me around, so I keep out of her way. Sometimes I hide from her, OK?'

'But why don't you like her?'

'It's not that I don't like her, it's just that, sometimes, she seems sort of desperate.'

'Mmmm.'

‘What does “Mmmm” mean?’ I asked.

‘Well, you need to have friends, Holly.’

I didn’t respond to that, we’d had the ‘friends’ chat loads of times.

‘Anyway, I feel sorry for her,’ mam went on.

‘Sorry for her? Why?’

‘Her eyes are too old.’

You see, sometimes adults really do hit it on the head. That was exactly right, Samantha’s eyes were definitely too old and I didn’t like them burrowing into me. There was a moment there, when mam said that, there was a second when I nearly blurted it all out. Jack, the pigs, Mrs Plum’s blood, the lot. But I didn’t, thank goodness. I did say I’d have a mug of cocoa, though, and mam put her arms around me to bring us close. I leant into her, glad to feel safe again, and she pressed right on the spot where I’d bruised myself banging into Mrs Plum’s bedroom door when she shouted at me.

I said ‘Ouch’ without thinking, and sure enough mam made me lift my pyjama top up so she could see where I was hurt.

‘How did this happen?’ she asked, staring at the bruise.

‘Playing football at playtime, I bumped into the goal-post.’ I was becoming very good at lying.

‘Has someone looked at it?’

‘Oh yeah, the school secretary checked it out.’

‘It looks really sore to me, you’ve broken the skin. Tell

you what, you get into bed and I'll bring your warm drink up. How's that?'

'That'd be great.'

When she brought the cocoa to my bedroom she started talking about Antony again. How much she liked him, how funny he was, how she wanted him and me to get on with each other.

No question that it was serious and she expected me to be as happy about it as she was, but to me he was a stranger. A stranger who she wanted me to share my life with.

After she'd gone I couldn't get comfortable. I didn't like what was happening to me and mam and my thoughts kept drifting to Mrs Plum. The smell, the mess, how she'd probably been nasty to Jack all his life, and yet he was still really loving to her. The thought of having to clean her up all the time, feed her, carry her up and down stairs did my head in. I wasn't sure I'd be able to do all that for my mam, yet Jack did it willingly and didn't seem to blame her for anything. And here was me still hoping that mam and Antony would split up, even though she was obviously happy with him.

Too restless to sleep, I went downstairs, got the tarot pack and took it to my bedroom. Laying the pack out, I tried to settle my mind with some deep breathing. This time I didn't ask a question, just let fate take control. The card I selected was 'The Empress'. The image showed a woman sitting on a throne. In her right hand she's holding a ceremonial rod, she has a crown on her head and two strings of pearls around her neck. She stares straight ahead. The first finger on her left hand points upwards. All around her there are trees and things growing, like corn. I checked the interpretation:

> *This card represents the emergence of the female archetype. It suggests using care and love to solve a problem rather than force. The Empress wants the best for those under her wing and is sometimes seen as a great mother figure and sometimes as a teacher or guide. She is loving and compassionate and willing to sacrifice a great deal in order to help others.*

I looked up 'archetype' in the dictionary:

> *The original pattern from which copies are made; a prototype.*

So, it was definitely something to do with becoming a woman, with growing up. There should be a manual on changing from childhood to being an adult. How does everyone go from insecure teenager to mature person able to hold down a job, run a house, do food stuff etc. But it's not as simple as that, is it? Look at mam, it's like she's the adolescent while I'm attempting to be grown up.

I ended up sleeping through my alarm in the morning and mam had to come and give me a shake. As I rushed into the kitchen I didn't notice her opening my rucksack to put my packed lunch in until it was too late. She went all silent, and when I looked she was holding up the *Chinese Horoscopes* book that Jack had let me borrow to read about the Year of the Pig.

She asked me where I got it and her voice was very clipped. I didn't stop to think, just stupidly blurted out that it was from the school library. Her eyes narrowed as she pointed out there was no library sticker. Then I 'remembered' I'd borrowed it but that wasn't enough for her, she wanted to know the who, the where and the when. It was as if all the closeness we'd had the night before had evaporated.

'What's your problem, mam? It's just a bloody book.'

The doorbell rang before she could respond but her face was tight with irritation. I rushed to answer it. So much for making friends again. It was a first for me, being pleased to see Samantha at the door, but mam barely acknowledged her arrival, just continued on about the flaming book. I couldn't understand what all the fuss was about.

'I'm waiting Holly. I want to know where you got this.'

There was no possible way she could know I'd got it from Jack, but still my stomach began churning up. Samantha did a little cough. 'It was me, Mrs Lock,' she said, 'Holly borrowed it off me.'

Mam was not convinced. She challenged both me and Samantha about telling the truth and then dropped her bombshell.

‘Well then, Samantha, maybe you can tell me how it comes to have the name “Daniel Plum” written on the title page?’

I went hot and cold in quick succession. Then I thought, hang on a minute, how does she know Jack’s dad’s name? So I asked her. She snapped at me not to try and change the subject. Fortunately, Samantha came up with a believable, if untrue, explanation.

‘I found it by the side of the Plums’ dustbin, Mrs Lock. I often go round on bin day to see if anybody’s throwing out anything good,’ she said quickly. She’s as sharp as an acid drop. I couldn’t help admiring her quick thinking.

Pursing her lips, mam turned her attention to me. She wanted to know why I hadn’t told her the truth in the first place.

I was lost for words. It wasn’t just being caught out, it was the fact that I now owed a favour to Samantha, who immediately took the opportunity to fill the space.

‘She was supposed to give it back to me, Mrs Lock – my dad wanted it – so she probably felt guilty,’ she cut in.

And then, thankfully, it was time for school and me and Samantha rushed out of the house. As soon as we got out of earshot she started on about how I didn’t have a clue how to deal with my mam, like there was one specific method.

‘Listen, you don’t argue,’ she said, ‘that’s pointless, you just tell parents what they want to hear, it’s so much easier.

Smile, tell them what fab parents they are, say yes to any suggestions they make, say sorry all the time, then do exactly what you want, and tell lies, the bigger the better. They want to believe that they've brought you up to be a fabulous person, because that means they've been great parents. Doesn't matter how many times you have to do it, it always works, tell them what they want to hear. Okay?'

She linked arms all the way to school and when we passed Paula Tompkins with some other girls, Samantha completely ignored her. Part of me was glad to have Samantha back, especially with mam in romance land, but another part wasn't. She'd be on my case all the time, watching, hanging about. I had Jack to protect and I didn't need Samantha breathing down my neck.

Unfortunately, in between maths and history, she crept up behind me in the corridor and made me jump. It was all I could do to stop myself slapping her.

'Anyway,' she said, 'you still going into Pardes Wood? You owe me a favour, so you've got to tell what you do in there. Are you meeting a lad? Come on, tell me. Don't leave me out of things, please, not now we're best friends again.'

I was grateful for her getting me out of the row with mam, so I promised to talk on the way home from school, but she was very persistent, as usual. She put her arm around my shoulder and pulled me too close. 'You got that book off Jack Plum, didn't you?' she whispered. Her breath was sour, like she hadn't brushed her teeth, and her eyes were glittering with triumph. I pulled free of her and took a deep breath.

THIRTEEN

Memories of dad the hog

The boxy room is as a stranger. I did not make a visit for many a long time. I get proper startles at beginning seek the ScrapBook, for how much of dad's things linger on here. His smell is up on them, as an old pipe knocked out, sweet with some sourness after. There is clothes, shoes, books, music, and between place, even the old writing book of dad's time. I am in memory that he put words into it. It is of a ripe plummy leather with a golden colour up on the page edges. I stroke on the words he writed long time back with the especial pen of bright bluebell inks, given from his own mammy. I stare to dad's own slanty small writing and I find some words I make recognitions of – 'pig', 'wood', 'water' – but lots of no knowledge. Dad showed to me the time telling and the numbers to fifty but made only small beginnings of words and readings before his going. Much after that I did get words from mam and listening at the radio.

I sniff at the book and plop it inside to my pocket, warm

dad words aside me. I make plans to ask Holly Lock to read from it when I am strong within my emotions. This scent of dad makes a sadglad thing for me. I do not want to be within it much long. Below of the creaky bed I find a woody box with jewels and beyond, the grassy patterns of ScrapBook is underlying. I do not look within, I know there is photos lurking. I will see all with Holly and the pigs close in to keep me safe from the frights.

I shut the door up on the dad fragrance, and so I can not dwell on things past and beyond. I take warm water within mam's room and softly wash her into a cleanness. Her eyelids is flappy as moths but not opening full and the skin is cool, as she has been within a breeze. I try and make talk with her but nothing does come back, excepting a touch up on my hand with one cold finger. Her mouth will not take food, even mashy porridge with much of treacle. The warmed up whisky I give seeps at the corners of her flopping lips.

I think Holly is in correctness about the dying and frighteners rush me, shaking me toes to hoghead as some windy scarecrow. They is always about, always waiting to get on the inside and without my pigs to run to, what would become this trembling fear? Would I shiver full loose? Would all space inside my cavern head fill up of blood things what bring no rest, no peace? If they take me from Holly and the pigs, the end will not arrive soon enough, but the worry is if my buried nobble of rage bursts out into hurt of others. I know that it could, I see it waiting in corners.

Mam must stay in some alertness for the doctor visit next daytime other wise he will think on hospitals and sending hogboy off, maybe to a cage or a dim room, ever far from earthy scents and piglove and Holly and Palace life and times. I must make proper wishes and offerings on this for it could sign the full end of all good things here. And as I do think on this there is a ringing at the doorbell that full startles me for I have not heard this in long times and I do cry out on its screeching around the house space. Then I crouch in stillness, pressing up on the wall and it does come an other time.

They is not leaving so I do slither along wall space to the downsteps window what looks over the gate path. As I reach at the curtain side there comes a rattling up on the door. I think the outside people is come and my breath gets full tight and ragged. Then, I see the postalman stroll the path putting curious glances at the up windows. After he is off away it takes much time for my heart to stop its blamming.

Up on the floor below the box for letters the postalman has plopped something. It is card with red and black words what look important and what put worry on me with their invasion.

In the Palace I sway and sing to put the frighteners far off. Freya and the tribe do their sweet whisper humming at me, they know it will bring the placids. When I listen full on at them I see soft meadowlands scattered of glossy flowers and peacock blue water running. The sky in that place comes violet and carries two suns, one marigold, one silvered. Many pigs dwell there, with humanpigkind what is naked of clothes but full with long fur, and they live without frighteners and without butchers. Pigs is free and uneaten. I wonder if this is pig dream they conjure for me, or pig memory of what is or was in an other place, maybe an other time?

Holly comes direct from school time and I am at the mild place, with all the pigstuff sinked in me. She plays the sweet flute and then we talk on death things. It is full strange, to estimate at the afterness of life when the body gets ended. I did see pig bodies beyond the ending, some of my tribe and others. Farmer Cotton does all ways take these off beyond the farlands in his motor lorry and in past times I did fetch any dead pigs at his holding place. With the dying I know some thing is gone, some thing what was as fire, as sun energy. Dad called this soul. Like the body is the flesh trolley what carries fire around and without the fire is nothingness.

I show to Holly the postalman card and she reads with carefulness.

'There's a letter that's got to be signed for,' she tells.

'What letter? From where?'

'It doesn't say. It just says they'll try again tomorrow or

you can go and collect it or have it delivered to your local post office.'

'What is best?'

She thinks on this some. 'Well, they need your mam's signature, so if I'm here in the morning when the post comes, I can open the door, get the thing to sign and pretend to take it up to your mam who's ill in bed. Then I'll just go up to the landing, sign it and bring it back.'

'That is good, Holly.'

'You'll have to keep watch at the window before I open the door and when I come back downstairs, right?'

'Right. And maybe it could be from dad, this what has to get signed for, do you think?'

'I don't know, Jack, but I really, really hope so.'

'He would not stop Holly being friend to me and pigs.'

'I'm sure he wouldn't.'

I tell Holly mam is worse and question if she will look on her again. I say of my doctor worries on the tomorrow. She makes agreement though I gather in that she has no eagerness to greet the stink of mam or her hate full words and I do not blame that. There is a trembling stillness all within the house as we creep upsteps to mam's room and I think I hear of small whispers up behind the wall spaces. Holly does stay at the door and I go in closeness to mam.

'Mrs Plum?' Holly calls, 'Mrs Plum?' There is no return sound from mam and Holly moves closer at me.

Mam's mouth is full open one side and she is untoothed.

Her eyes stare but do not see. I touch mam's hand, to make comfort, it is cold as ice puddles in deep wintering time. Holly touches too and she gives a quick cry and jumps back. She looks at me then with danger eyes and I do notice her hands get trembly and her breath sucking in.

'I . . . I think she's dead, Jack,' she says after some space, and there is a throbbing inside her words.

I do not want to hear of death so I shake at mam's body and shout her to wake up. I want to shake breath within her, some live breath, and I do shake so hard the bed does jump from up the floor and makes crash sounds. I feel something as a moth way far within my stomach. It flutters quick right within my throat, and begins to choke and I have to howl great long and loud to get it gone. And then Holly is slapping at me and calling my name out as in a dream tunnel and she does make pinches on my hoghands to fetch me to see and hear her.

'Stop it, Jack! Stop it!' she does yell out and she throws water up at my face from mam's nighttime glass and I do then take notice and stop the shaking of the bed. I see I has shaked mam right into the end of it and nearly to the floor space. After that tears come and Holly presses her quaking hands at mam's wrists and shakes her head.

'Mrs Fisher showed us how to do it in First Aid,' she tells me, 'taking the pulse. It's just to be sure, Jack.'

There is no pulsing. The floor is feathers and I wobble. I shout of Holly what we will do. It is disaster stuff. The frighteners could get me in full grip now and they would never flee. The shivering and snorting starts and seems to drag me off away from the room to some full white place of no windows and no doors and all I hear is rattlings, as a snake what is in one of my pig books. Then, in and about the rattle is sob sounds and I do see outside of the whiteness is Holly sat full rigid within mam's wheelchair. Her lips is apart and sucking of the air and her teeth is knocking sharp, as the lids on her eyes do flutter real wild. Deep down within the cellar space comes Freya and the older tribe sows calling at me, calling for soothing to send off the frightener's grip. I listen and take breath and let quiet pig-song come in to me.

Holly is extreme cold in her shivering. I place clean blankets all about her and wheel her away from the death stench. Then I carry her up over the shoulder down to the Palace for pig loving and sweet tea for comforting. And later, when some calm is within her and me, she does long sighings.

'Are you okay, Jack?' she says in whisper words.

'I am shaked up, Holly, as it did come too sudden up on me. I did think on her dying but not really know of it and she did not make goodbye to me.'

'She couldn't, Jack, but there's things you can do, like rituals. You have to tell things to your mam,' she says. 'I've read all about it. Like you're making your goodbyes, sending her off to another place. Some people think that the spirits of dead people linger on in this world until they've had a chance to say goodbye. We have to make sure she goes. So, go on up there, Jack, say things, tell her stuff you would have liked her to know.'

'No, cannot go up there alone, the frighteners is waiting on me, to grab and take me off.'

'I don't think I can walk up, Jack, but if you carry me, I'll come with you. I'll sit in the wheelchair just outside the door, will that help?'

And this is what we do and I do slow my head down and look inside it for things I might make up for mam and I find a whole surprising shelf full. 'Pigs take three months, three weeks and three days to be born, mam,' I say. Holly nods and I know I am doing correct. 'They make differing sounds, mam, as sad, happy, full of joy, hooligan, angry, and they get Deep pression too, as you. Dad told this all before he left. They can die full out of stress, these are some true things about pigs. I did rear them, mam, and now you will not know ever of my cleverness in that and you will not tell me where dad did go or say he is hog no more.' I stop to find more words.

'He was a good son to you,' Holly says, 'and you should have treated him better than you did.'

'Some times she could get nice,' I say.

'Okay, sometimes you were nice, but not often.'

'Goodbye, mam,' I start up again. 'No more pain or bloodcoughing. No more of my bad breath on you, turning you to enrage. Maybe there will be whisky where you are gone . . . maybe not, but you do get free of me and my big boar's head now.'

'Amen,' Holly says.

'Amen,' I say. And frights rushes in to close my throat off from air

'You mustn't panic, Jack,' Holly says. 'I don't know what I'll do if you crack up. Take deep breaths, please. We've got to think, we've got to make a new plan.'

'Of what?'

And then she does make reminder to me of the doctor visit next daytime and all else we must make preparations for. Thinking on it sends me quiet and breath comes in as a panting canine's. Holly takes on extreme serious looks and comes out from the wheelchair to pace around as a stud bull does.

'Open the windows, Jack,' she says and I see she does struggle with a jumpy throat what could bring vomits on. 'And let's go back down to the Palace. My brain won't work up here and I think I can walk now.'

It is like Holly does have whisky taken into her. She has come extreme fast at talk and her eyes do come a bit stary. 'First, Jack,' she says, when we is settled among our tribe, 'nobody must know she's dead.'

When I ask on the doctor visit she breathes sharp in as when pain comes and then she makes pacing, downup, downup, and small mumblings and my throat does fill up as cement, all cloggy at dread of what might come. But my voice does squeeze through in a grumbly way to ask Holly to stop the outsidepeople splatting all my Palace away.

'Stop that moaning, Jack. I'm trying to keep things together and you've got to help by keeping quiet.'

I make big efforting and do what Holly tells.

'Okay then, apart from the doctor, every so often, nobody ever comes here. You collect her pension. If you keep doing that, things can just go on as they are and if something crops up, like this letter that's got to be signed for, or like the doctor, we'll find a way of dealing with it. We will, Jack, you have to believe that. But you mustn't get panicky, it'll make things worse. I'm just as scared as you are but we have to be strong.'

I get slow to what Holly is thinking. It will be as pretending. We make the pretend that mam is live flesh and no body will come to take me off. Yes, it is a good way and I thank the god of pigs for Holly.

'Yes, Holly,' I say then, 'we can make the pretend thing.'

She begins extra pacing up down the room. She has more of the thinking to do. I wait. I think on mam in her stillness as I might believe she is in the whisky sleep. Holly stops the walk about and looks at me pointy and I know something more is to come.

'Right. The doctor. We have to clean your mam's room up, fresh sheets, everything. Then we have to put your mam's body somewhere . . . oh God, the body, I don't know if I can do this, Jack, I don't know if I can cope.' She looks a question at me with eyes what seem sunked in and lips what is with wobbles and I scour at solution thoughts.

'We can do, Holly, I will keep off frighteners for helping. Promise.'

'Don't you mind . . . touching her . . . cleaning her . . . cleaning everything?' Holly says with some disgust feelings up on her.

'I do it all ways when she is live . . . so . . . there will be no splatting or cursing on me now and that will be some ease. I have telled the hoghead it must come strong, it must follow what Holly says. That is the only way, the pretend way, to stay with pigs.'

'I couldn't do it, Jack. I've never seen a dead body before, apart from our old dog, and it's frightening. One minute there's life, next minute nothing. How scary is that?'

'Not your mam, Holly, not your life and your pig's lives needing of protection. I can do.'

'Okay then. I'll come first thing in the morning and phone the surgery and give some excuse why the doctor can't come. I'll say your mam's had to visit a relative in . . . in Durham. That you've taken her on the train in the wheelchair.'

'I could not do . . . mam would not go outsidetime with me . . .'

'It's pretend, Jack, remember?'

My senses is well disturbed at all this death and new

planning and I must shake the hogskull to keep the focusing. Holly does still pace and make the plans but there is a weakening within and her voice does have a new, unhappy sound.

'But,' she tells on, 'even if they believe me, they'll want to make another appointment straight off, won't they?' She makes tutting and phewing out her mouth. It is hard to make up good plans when you is scared up. 'So, we have to say she's away for weeks and weeks to give us more time. Could she pretend to visit your grandparents?'

'All dead and gone to Jee Sus.'

Holly says some swearing words and I dread of more frights coming up on her. She walks and stops and turns and thinks and all the time of it I hear cracked whisperings from all about and mam's breathing no more. Then Holly full startles me with a clap of hands.

'I've got it, Jack,' she tells, and there is some little relieving on her. 'You'll phone up the surgery!'

I think she has lost senses at this but she squeezes at my arm for reassuring.

'It's perfect, Jack. You'll phone using your mam's voice. You don't stutter when you do that, so it'll be fine. I'll be with you, listening on the phone, and I'll be able to tell you what to say. It'll work, I know it will. First we'll tell them she has to visit a sick auntie in . . . somewhere further than Durham . . . mmm . . . Scotland, that's it. Then we'll ring again later and say she's decided to go and live with her. It happens all the time, Jack. I can remember mam sorting it all out for Gran and Grandad Logan.'

Even in her raggedness from the stench of death stuff, Holly has made a solving as I never would or could and I am grate full and less frighted.

'We can't just leave her body, though, Jack.' I see how the mind of her does never stop its working. 'Dead things smell bad.'

'Maggots,' I say, because I did see it on dead birds and rabbits within Pardes Wood.

'Don't talk about maggots, please.' Her words come croaked up and she does run for the tap to get water, which she slurps as a hungry piglet. Freya follows and gives a soft rubbing at her side, then Peach and some of the piggylets run to press their snouts at her.

'You is not good, Holly, time to go to home maybe?'

'Don't think I could walk that far yet and I think I'll feel better if we've sorted some things out before I go home.'

'Right. So if we bury . . .' I start but she makes the interrupt.

'Burying's no good . . . how far could we take the body? Someone might see us . . . or the body might be found. It's too risky, Jack, I've seen it loads of times on TV. They always discover the body.'

I wonder who 'they' can be but speedy I know – it is those who would keep 'monsters' off the streets and locked up in indoor places.

'You must practice imitating your mother's voice straightaway, Jack, so that you can do it really well.'

I promise, though I know I can do it in perfection. My pigs have witness to conversationing with her and me in the Palace, but of only myself.

'And I'll practise her signature, for the pension book and anything else that crops up. Okay?'

I do nod. Holly pushes her lips together tight as if she holds in the fright of the death behind her teeth. We do stare to each other like we is lost.

'I'm not sure we can carry all this off, Jack. My brain doesn't seem to be listening to me, it just keeps trying to make me go to sleep. What about you?'

'I is extreme tired but also carry a screeching noise within my ears what I know will not let me sleep.'

'We must be in shock, Jack. It affects people in different ways. Will you be all right if I go home?'

I nod the okay and we do rest eyes on our pinched up faces. I have no grasping on solutions. Holly sighs and for some small seconds extreme quiet comes up on us so I hear the ticktocking clock upsteps. Freya and the pigs do make silent tribe closeness at us. No thing stirs excepting Holly's canine breathing until, in the nearby distances, Samantha makes the calling out on Holly's name far off in the upoutside and we do both get the startles, as it is a full reminder of outsidepeople.

Holly's upsetness does make a weakening within me, like

there is an opening coming into my hogbody what I could get swallowed in. But I keep strong in voice and looks so as not to fright her more.

'I'll think about the body,' she says.

'I should do the wash of mam? To make a readiness for the . . . the . . .'

'Yes, wash her, Jack, and put on clothes that she liked, as if she was going on an important journey, right? I've got to get out of here but I'll be back here in the morning at eight and we'll do the phone call and sort out that letter. Is that okay?'

'You is sure you will come, Holly? You will not do the abandoning as . . . as dad did?'

She makes a big squeeze on my hoghands and does promise on her returning and I do let her sneak to outside after certainness of no Samantha sighting.

Way back down within the Palace, absent of Holly, a gloom thing comes up on me, a burdening gloom for me to stay close with the pigs. I stay in among my tribe until time for nighttrotting when I cry soft at the navy blue sky and the pigs proddle the water and grass. Mam is gone. I am full alone with my pigs. I am afeared of Holly getting full into frights and not able to come to us and I am full afeared of the blood, stink, puke, mess of what was mam could drive Holly off to safeness and away from the Freak. If she does not come for the doctor thing I is full doomed. On all these thoughts I make a fight but I do not go back to that room of death until dawnlight comes. Then I sing favourite songs as I make preparations of mam's empty flesh trolley what will chase her soul to some next place, where we might collide up some future time.

After, I do toetip to the boxy room, for aloneness away from death space. I gaze at morningtime's arrival up on all. The light of it, the warm of it, gliding and glistering along tree branches, grass, puddles, fetching the lifeglow what is from sun energies for all our living. Round near by the river place, the trees is thick in together and full blossomed. The flowers is mouth wide as if calling tunes to the day coming. There is a silver mist remnant gliding upward for mingling in to the cornflower blueness of sky. Maybe this is soul stuff, energy soul stuff, rising at a forever rest place. In the case it is I whisper of goodbyes and make a small wave and I do breathe deep in the scent of dad which is still strong in that space.

FOURTEEN

Holly Lock's world

It was like touching cold lard – no, more like a soft, icy candle. Mrs Plum didn't feel human, there was no life in her hand. And the sour smell was almost overwhelming, sort of bitter but with traces of something too sweet. It was hard to breathe because the room felt airless, like all the oxygen had been sucked up by the dead body in one last effort to hold on to life. Somehow she was more frightening dead than when she was alive, but I kept thinking she'd suddenly lurch back and lash out at me with her bloody fingers. I never really thought about it before, but what Jack said about the body being something for the soul to travel about in, that made sense when I touched Mrs Plum's lifeless hand.

A dead body lying in Jack's house and I couldn't tell anyone or ask for help either. Unless they'd listen to me. Would they listen to me, the doctors, the social workers, or would they just drag him off to some 'care facility' without sight of a field, never mind a pig? Somehow I couldn't see them allowing Jack to stay on in the house with his pigs and I couldn't see them getting him a little smallholding to live on, things just don't work like that. Anyway, there was nothing I could do without Jack's agreement, that wouldn't be fair, it was his choice. I was slightly crazy thinking about it all, the body, the lies, the doctor, the postman, Samantha on my back, mam off with her boyfriend.

My head was throbbing by the time I got home but I forced myself to try and hold it all in, push it to the back of my mind, just to get through the next day. I didn't do very well, because mam got in early and she picked something up straightaway when she caught me slumped on the sofa, staring into space. If I'd known she'd be early I'd have dragged myself up to my room.

'What's wrong?' she said, in her 'concerned' voice.

I climbed off the sofa to go upstairs because I didn't know how much of her probing I could handle. My insides felt like a wave machine had been switched on. Mam got in front of me and blocked the doorway. She told me not to walk out when she was trying to talk. She had this pouty, hurt look, a bit like one of Samantha's 'poor misunderstood me' expressions and suddenly it all came tumbling on top of me. Mrs Plum's death, Jack's fear of being sent away, not feeling I could trust Samantha, and mam, expecting me to just accept this guy into my life.

'Leave me alone,' I said.

'I beg your pardon –,' she began, but I cut her off by

pushing her sideways. She was stronger than I expected, she stumbled but kept her balance and surged towards me with her arm outstretched. I realised she was going to slap me so I kicked at her ankles and made contact with her shin. She yelped and as I tried to get past her to the door she grabbed my sweatshirt and we struggled so fiercely we both ended up on the floor. I was shouting at her to get off me and leave me alone and fighting to keep the tears at bay when she suddenly pinned me on the ground. Her breath was being forced out of her nose like an exhausted horse.

'What is wrong with you?' she asked breathlessly.

I wanted to shout back at her, 'I've just touched a dead body, that's what's wrong with me', but instead I just latched on to something she might listen to. 'I'm sick of you getting at me and expecting me to see things your way. You treat Samantha better than you treat me.'

'I don't,' she said, loosening her grip on me a little.

'You invited her to my party when I didn't want her there.'

'It seemed cruel to leave her out when she's been coming to your parties since she was a baby.'

'But you said I could choose.'

Sighing, she screwed up her face, like she was thinking hard, then let go of my sweatshirt and dropped on to the floor beside me.

'Okay, you're right. I'm sorry about that, I should have let you choose.'

'And this morning, when you were going apeshit about that book, you believed everything she said but kept thinking I was lying.'

'I didn't believe her straightaway, that's not fair, but I suppose I did make too much of a fuss about the book.'

She must have seen the tears flooding into my eyes because she put her arm around me and I didn't pull away. Resting my head on her shoulder, I let the tears come. We must have made a peculiar sight, lying there on the floor. Mam held me tight until the tears stopped then got me some tissues, pulled me to my feet and guided me to the sofa.

'You feeling ill again?' she asked.

'I'm just tired and Samantha's been buggin' me all day.'

She must have picked up my reluctance to talk because she just stroked my hair until I was nearly asleep. It all felt so safe and reassuring until the sound of the phone brought me back to reality.

Mam eased herself off the sofa to answer it. The tone of her voice told me it was Antony. My limbs were too weak for me to get upstairs and I felt sort of exposed sitting there on my own, so I pulled the loose cushions off and made a bed on the floor between the wall and the back of the sofa. Then I curled up into a ball to sleep.

I was just sinking into a dream where Jack was running into Pardes Wood with all the pigs, carrying his mam's body on his shoulders, being chased by a group of men in suits, when mam touched my shoulder to wake me. She was startled by my reaction, which was to shout 'No!' and retreat further behind the sofa, until I realised where I was.

'Steady on, sweetheart,' she said. 'You just dropped off, everything's all right.'

I wished it was. My neck was stiff, my head was beginning to throb and mam was looking at me with such sympathy that I hated myself for deceiving her. The best thing was to get away from her before I said something I'd regret. That's the trouble with lies, they can catch you out. I told her I'd be better after a bath and an early night. Instead of looking pleased she seemed disappointed.

She followed me upstairs and sat on my bed while I got the bath running. I could tell there was something she wanted to say, something she was having difficulty with. It's strange, you don't expect adults to have problems finding the right words. It happens to me all the time, then later, when I'm on my own I'll be kicking myself for making a mess of things. I decided to help her out.

'You don't have to stay in, mam. I'm not ill, I'll be perfectly all right on my own.' It wasn't true, of course. I wanted her to stay in, to sit on my bed until I fell asleep, to be near by in case I had nightmares about Mrs Plum.

It came out then. Antony had booked a table for us all at Sorrento's. They'd decided it was time for me and him to meet. Bad timing, mam. What about checking with me first? Worse than that, she went into her room and came back with a short, sleeveless, black fitted dress with Chinese embroidery on the collar.

I told her that even if I'd felt like going out, which I didn't, I'd look like a plank in that sort of dress, which she knew I'd say really. But still she tried to get me to try it on and stressed that it was a designer label, as if I cared. All I could think of was that she must be ashamed of the way I normally looked. As far as I was concerned I'd been more than reasonable, so why couldn't she just go out and leave me alone? Biting back my irritation I asked her to let me have my bath and get to bed but she wouldn't let it go. Antony would be disappointed; Antony would be expecting us; Antony bloody this and that. That did it for me.

'Mam, you're not listening to me, again. Just go out. I don't want to meet Antony. I like things the way they are, just you and me on our own.'

Her response was the big dramatic sigh, then silence. Why couldn't she just drop it? She was making me feel less and less sympathetic. If someone doesn't listen to what you say, what are you supposed to do?

'Antony's part of my life now, Holly, and that means he's going to be part of yours. Before long you'll be up and grown and leaving home. You'll have boyfriends of your own, probably even get married. I have to think about my future.'

'It's not like he's moving in with us, is it?' The flicker of her eyelids was enough to answer my question.

I walked into my bathroom and locked the door. She knocked and tried to get me to come out but I ignored her. All my energy was draining away. I slid down the wall and hit the floor with a bump. I must have sat there for twenty minutes, sobbing quietly, until I heard her leave the house.

I climbed into the cooling bath, topped it up with hot water and tried to soak all the tension away, lying with my head under the water to deaden any sound. It helped, a bit, but when I was putting my pyjamas on I began to feel dizzy. Wrapping myself in my duvet I let my eyes close. I was desperate for sleep but as I began to drop off, all the stuff about Mrs Plum started boiling my brain. Because just suppose we pulled off the doctor thing, what the hell were we going to do with the body?

I knew it was up to me to find solutions. After all, there was nobody else I could turn to for help, unless we could somehow locate Jack's dad. That was what I clung on to as I lay in bed listening to the distant sound of a train rumbling through the night, that Mr Plum might be found and brought home.

I had no stomach for the tarot but I did get out of bed and talk to my plants. Lots of people do it. They're living things after all, and without plants and trees Planet Earth would be in a bad way, lack of oxygen for a start. My lemon geranium was the most receptive, its leaves seemed to quiver and lean towards me. Or maybe I was just slowly losing my mind with all the trauma. Anyway, I told them everything, laid it all out and in some peculiar way, I did feel better afterwards. Just as my eyes began to close at last, I wondered how Jack was coping with it all. At least he had the comfort of Freya and the others.

FIFTEEN

Slugs and snails

The house space is much changed, like it was shuddered up at mam's soul leaving. I hear more whisperings within walls and some times small squashed cries of hurt come up between floor boards. I think it is of memories or regret what have snared and meshed with wood and brick. I also forget to feed with the whiff and taste of the death room and echo of the times long past whisperings slithering about.

Holly is with us earlytime as agreed, before school and doctor surgery opening. She has writed down some begin words and she helps hoghead to learn and repeat of them.

Good morning, may I speak to Doctor Taylor, please? This is Mrs Plum from number one River Street. I'm afraid I have to cancel your visit this morning . . .

And so it does go on. I am full tremble at the prospect as I never did the phone talk past times. But Holly sits in closeness and listens in at the ear of it and she does whisper reply words within my own ear extreme clear.

'We did it, Jack,' she says at phone down.

'Yes, Holly,' I say in my pleased up voice, 'you is one amazingful piggirl.'

The words is out of my hogmouth one second only and the bell rings for the door. I look to Holly and she does nod. It is postalman. I do my window check for all to be quiet as Holly walks for the door. At my yes nod she opens. There is some words and she goes upsteps on the pretend thing of mam signing his card. All is done good, street checked, letter got, door closed up in only few minutes but Holly remains stuck at the door. The letter does quiver within her titch hand and I move in closer for the light to show her face. It is lost of brightness.

'What?' I do ask.

'Oh Jack, nothing's going right. Mrs Robson, from the shop, was just coming out of the wood with her dog as I closed the door. She saw me.'

This is not good. Mrs Robson knows this is hoghouse.

'Have a look, see if she's gone, I'm going to be late for school again.'

When I comes from checking up the road, Holly does have the special letter open and I tell from her face it is not of dad's sending.

'It's from some insurance company, Jack. It says your mam had a policy with them and now she gets a dividend or something. They've got a cheque for her, five thousand pounds, and . . .' She stops the words to pull at her breath. 'Oh no, they're sending someone here in person because they have to witness your mam's signature. That's all we bloody need, Mrs Robson and now this.'

'We could tell it is not wanted.'

'I don't think it works like that. Nobody would turn down five thousand pounds. They'll phone before they come, though, so that's something.'

'I do not answer phone.'

'That's probably best.'

'Will Mrs Robson tell of you, Holly?'

'Mam only goes in the shop at weekends, but it's Thursday today so that only gives us two days. Mrs Robson's a right gossip, though, so she might tell someone else. Christ-all-bloody-mighty, Jack, why can't anything go right for us? It's not fucking fair, we haven't done anything wrong. I'll just have to nip out of school at morning break and make up some story for Mrs Robson, something that'll stop her gabbing. God knows what like.' Her body does slump until her watch is checked. 'I've got to go, Jack. Don't worry, I'll see you later.'

Some times, when the frighteners and dread is strongest, they hiss to me that I will change to pigkind, that soon trotters will burst through feetskin and my back will bend for the ground and my face will sprawl into snout. And bits of hogbrain wonder if that would be so unwanted: to roll and rumble with sweet porkers; to mudlark, wallow, guzzle to my full desire. Until Blandish the butcher and his human-pigkind comes inside the picture, all scraping, screeching steel and chopping blocks and muscly arms and aprons full splattered of blood and guts and shattered bone.

My sorrow thoughts on Holly and what I did bring up on her, with a dead mam and all that, do gather up and around me all the day hours but I do make the frights keep back by thinking strong on dad. Mam's body does already smell putridly, as cupboards never opened does. It drifts down banisters wherever I go, like the awful reek of the long past, leaning heavily on the now and future times. And each single car what stops near by I almost hear a gong clonking inside my stretched tight skin. With that and the whisperings, I quake I will come undone, that Holly Lock might get frights and tell of death what lies here. I would hold nil blame up on Holly. I would understand much that her world is out there, it is where she must full time live and breathe.

Holly Lock does not come to the Palace immediate after school as is getting the usual and I have dread it might become abandonedment time. It is like I know the truth of aloneness. My pigs is every thing, yes, but humanpigs come differing, as my sort of beast, whether they, or me, like it. Once I had dad, then only mam, and later it was Holly to humansize my outlooks. If Holly will not come . . . if she gets scared off with the trepidations, because of the body-death . . .

I stop the hoghead from this dread by doing extreme cleaning of mam's room. I do put her body within the bath, all blanketed up and washed. I did do my best at her preparations. Then I fetch all sheets, towels, nightclothing, socks, under pants into bin bags all knotted up tight. They will go to Farmer Cotton's rubbish burning pile. There is much dust, lots of dead insect creatures, sweetie wrappings, in all corners, but I do not stop until the gleams is every place. It will be a part in the rituals what Holly telled, this full cleanse.

The sky does lose light and still Holly does not come and the worryings come back at me with extra forcing. What if she will not ever come? What if Mrs Robson did make bad gossip on her? These words do spin at me badly and I need the sanctuary of pigspace extreme swift, if frighteners is not to see the gaps they could get within.

Freya and all is still in quietness after the upset of mam's dying. They is so attended to mine and Holly's miseries and moods, as if we really is of pig flesh. When I do begin my updown pacings to bash off the frighteners' spaces they make sweet hummings for my comfort. Within my hogskull I make many repeats of Holly's name. I do not want her caught up in more dangers. I think extreme hard on the magic of pigrelicstone, making the picture of it within the core textspace of my brain and I say hopes that it will not abandon me to the outsideworld people.

My hoghead does throb madly and there is burning all

up on my shoulder places and deep hurt up on my chest, pushing, pushing at me and I think I must howl to be free from this crushing. Then, like it is in dreamtime, I hear the small feet triptropping the Palace downsteps, bringing outside life to my space, which is good and bad. I want to snug her and swing her in the air for the joy of her return but I must not touch. I remember that from dad. He was extreme about it.

'You mustn't forget that you're much stronger than others, Jack,' he said. 'You can't play games like the normal kids do because in your excitement you might hurt someone. Best to keep your distance, Jack. Always keep your distance.'

And I do as he told. Even though my heartspace does thunder with the wanting-to-hug feelings I keep distance all ways. But she does see within my hurts as she is now pigwise.

'What is it, Jack? You look awful, are you hurt?' I tell of the crushing and her eyes does get extreme crackly. 'Where's the pain, is it here?' And she does place her titchy hand below my chest space where my heart does blam. I nod and do lay back into hay for resting.

Holly fetches new water for me and holds it at my hogmouth in quivery hands. She is afeared for me and I am extreme touched from this tender stuff.

'Maybe we should ring the doctor, Jack, get someone to check you out,' she says.

I tell her the blamming is moving off me and the pain does come less, which is truth, and perhaps it is from her coming. I don't tell of my fears on abandonment, she is filled up enough of worryings. She does give big sighings and plops next my hogbody up on the hay and we do lie as wood planks, side on side in stillness and full surrounded by tribe mutterings and snorts.

'I'm sorry I was late, Jack, I have to be extra careful with Samantha on my case all the time,' she says soon. 'And I went home after school to have a shower and get my things.' She holds up a boxy thing of red leather and makes grinning. 'I'm gonna stay the whole night with the pigs.'

Firstly I think on the good of it to me, for me, Holly and every pig to be all in together, but slowly, it does rattle in the hogskull how it should not be. The mams will come looking, they will gather others and they will come . . . I tell of this to Holly and she is in dumps.

'I thought we were friends, Jack,' she says. 'I don't want to go home, I want to stay here.'

Then comes the talk of the man her mam will squeeze inside their home and I think I understands the gloomies. She leans in up on me in her sad time and I wish to squash her into cheerfulness but fear of the hurting is greater so I do not. We talk on about this man and I promise if he becomes a full torment to Holly we will drive him off.

'What of Mrs Robson?' I ask then.

'I had a good idea for that. At lunchtime I went to the

shop and asked if she had any jobs which needed doing because I was getting points for a community medal by doing good deeds. She got me dusting shelves in her stock room and when I'd finished I just said, really casual, about how early she takes her dog out. Well, it took a few seconds to sink in but then, hello, she got the message. "Oh, that's what you were doing in Mrs Plum's house then, getting more points," she said. So, hopefully, if she blabs about me at all, it'll just be what a good girl I am.'

We splat hands and I is full amazed an extra time at the excellent brain system she has got.

My pains and hurt do go far off with this talk and for extra comforting I play with my throwing voice and sing, so extra soon Holly does get more smiles, until she does see mam's body brought downsteps, all blanketed up and ready, at the dark place by Pardes Wood pigexit.

'Why have you brought it down here, Jack?' she gasps extreme sharp.

'Because of my worries about smelling bodies and whisperings and flies that was all coming, loads, and someone passing could see suspicions in these flies. And you did say that mam's body must be got away.' Holly puts up an extreme serious face.

'You're right, Jack, it's going to be horrible very soon. Listen to this.' She pulls at some paper within a pocket and reads of the words she has put. '"Decomposition in the air is twice as fast as when a body is under water . . . the decomposing tissues release green substances and gas and the tongue may protrude . . ."'

This is the breaking apart and seeping of it, like I seen at Pardes Wood of dead creatures, it is full of putridness and horror. 'What must get done?' I say.

'It says, "a corpse can become a moving mass of maggots in twenty-four hours". Twenty-four hours, Jack, that's tonight. I don't want to see that, Jack, I couldn't take it.'

Holly has an ashy shade at her face and I do feel the vomity waves inside of me also.

'We've got to get rid of it, Jack.'

'Mam, Holly – why keep naming "it"?'

'Because it is an it, Jack. Your mam's gone now. Look at the body, feel it. I've read all about it and thought about it till my head feels as if it will burst. It's . . . it's just bones and meat now, I've checked it out. And remember what your dad said, about how the soul leaves?'

'Like . . . like carcass at butcher's shop?' I say, because I know of the truth in what she tells. I did see the death thing in the pig fields nearby and in my own piglings, I know what is. It is not good feeling but it is truth. Mam is gone. Nothing lingers which is true of her. Then Holly stares full at me in alertness. An other thought plan has come into her. This I know.

'Jack?' she says. And inmost her voice does lurk extreme worry from outsidetimes before full dark fall. My Pig Palace to be invaded by outside words and deeds, this is truth of what the fear fetches me, like I see clear on time to come.

'Yes?' I say with expectedness.

'Y'know when your dad worked for Blandish the butcher?'

'Yes?'

'Did he have his own butcher's tools?'

'He . . . yes . . . big knives . . . choppers . . . saws . . . why Holly?'

'Did he leave them behind when he left?'

Clang it goes inside hogskin and skull. The butchering thing swarming into Pig Palace. The bilge, blood, swill and slops of it all within this place.

'Jack?' Holly's voice comes from the foggy distance. 'Jack?' Like I slip off and away, tumbling in the frightener's space, which is unbounded with no exit place. I make huge efforts, like shake my hoghead, slap the skull and I make a clearing to come back and tell Holly dad did leave that stuff and I did keep them in clean shinyness in expectance of his return.

'You know what I'm thinking, Jack, don't you?' she asks and I do the slow nod nod. 'It's the only way to be sure . . . if you chop the body up and . . . and . . . Jack, will the pigs eat it? Do they eat that sort of thing?'

'They will eat . . . if I do ask . . . but . . . but I . . . I can not do butchering things, not here, not in Pig Palace . . . it would fetch much worry at them and I would see the mam within the butchering.'

Holly does not say one thing, her face is still extreme pearly as she is in deep anxious about the body and the maggots. I do drift into past places within to visit with the stink and stench in the back place of Blandish the butchers, red running blood, the slipperyness under the foots. And a memory slip of dad telling, 'They don't feel anything, Jack, they don't feel any pain, not once they're dead. It's the before time, the knowledge that they are going to die, that's the bad time.' But still, I am not ready for choppers and saws within the Palace. And I tell Holly I can not do it. I can not do the butchering of mam.

'I know, Jack. I'm sorry, it was a crazy thing to say, but my brain's burning up trying to sort everything out.'

There is a floppiness all about her, like she must lie down or she must fall, in her heart place is a tremor what shakes everything. Peach does leap at her for giving love and Holly wraps her up close in to her fluttery chest. I tell her that I is sorry she did get into this death and body removals. My plan of our connection was not of this but of good times of talk and nighttimepigtrotting and pig riding, not of this dread stuff.

'I've been thinking, Jack . . . maybe we need to get some help. I could talk to someone, get advice about what they might do if they find out your mam's dead.'

I shake my hoghead, but not harsh as I do not want more upset up on her. I tell she must go and find rest and some peacefulness and I will take mam's body deep in Pardes

Wood at deadnighttime and bury her close by pigrelicstone.

'I don't think so, Jack. What if someone sees you carrying the body into the wood? Like Samantha hanging about or someone taking a dog out, or someone who can't sleep, or a late poacher. It's too dangerous. And if they did find the body later – say some dog digs it up or a badger – they might think you killed her, or else why hide the body? Don't you see how difficult it is?'

I see she has spent much thinking time on this, for the help of me and she has good ideas about dangers. We go into a silent time again, only Peach and other piggylets giving snufflings into the air until Freya does snout me hard, pushing me at the cupboard and I remember of the ScrapBook and writing book. I pull them within my arms and take them for Holly.

'Is this the ScrapBook?' she asks.

I nod extreme fast, so glad to think on other things which is not so fear-making.

'And this.' I give to her the writing book.

'Well done, Jack, this might help us out. ScrapBook first, okay?'

She tries to give up calming even within her shakiness and we do sit side against side up on hay. Holly turns pages and I have no expectation of what is to be. The first off page has the picture of a massive baby covered full of fluffy white stuff.

'Jack, look, that's you!' Holly says. 'It says "Jack at six months".'

'Baby Jack of the big hogskull,' I say.

'You look cute, very cute. And this is your mam and dad,' she says, with the finger at the next page. 'It's their wedding, look at the clothes. Don't they look happy?'

We gaze up on the photo for some long time. I never saw mam and dad in happiness as that, except dream times, and I have to keep staring to put this full picture into memory space.

'What goes wrong, Jack? How can they be so happy and then . . .?'

I say that it was me what went wrong, me what made mam's ill stuff and caused the unhappiness and breakage.

'No, Jack, I didn't mean that. It's not just you, I've seen my mam's photos as well and dad and her look just like this but he left us too . . . that went wrong as well . . .'

Peach snuggles deeper at Holly, pressing her snout up on her arm. She knows the sadness and gives up love. The porky skin tickles and makes Holly laugh.

'Peach loves you,' I tell. 'Piggies are only ones ever love me.'

Holly turns pages over and shows more dad. 'That's not true, Jack. Look, look at the way your dad's looking at you. I think he loved you, look.'

'If he loved, why leave?' I ask. She turns more and more, reading of the papers and looking and I have knowing she is wanting answers there for me. I wait in quiet time until some thing stops the hand turn and Holly stares full at me with a cloud up on her face.

'Here, Jack,' she says with extreme hush. 'Here's the reason.'

I stare on the ScrapBook page. It is some thing not by hand, like pension books, but the words do not fit for me. 'What is it of, Holly? What are the words?'

There comes a deep sighing as she makes to speak. 'I'm really, really sorry, Jack . . .' she says, 'it's . . . it's not what I expected . . . it's a death certificate.'

'Death?' I speech it out too loud and she startles. This death thing was not with thoughts on dad, it is a mam thing.

Holly touches the big rough hand of me with her puny one. 'It says that your dad's dead, Jack. He didn't leave you at all. He was knocked down by a car and he died.'

This is a fat thought to take inside. Maybe too big, for there can be excessiveness of things, especial of death. The clang of it rattles within my hogskull and there comes a coldness up on my heart space. One dread thought blasts at me like hailstones: I do not want it. I do not want dad in death.

I stand up big as I can be and bellow this up on the Palace walls. Holly makes her massive eye stare and moves off from the hay and away further from the raging hog and into the comfort of pigs. I do bellow long and make huge stampings, fetching a dusty storm of hay. The hurt does grip at my chest, squeezing at my breath and soon I become wavy and much hot and do drop in weakness up on the bales. My heart space is blamming extreme loud and massive tears do river my face.

I can not move more as the weakness is full over me. I do put the pieces of it all together for the keeping and knowing within hogbrain.

'Mam knew he got dead?' I say, when my breath does come back.

'I'm sorry, Jack, but she must have done. She put all these things in this ScrapBook, didn't she?' Holly's voice comes at me wrapped in wool but I still hear what I hope not.

I think on that for some while, as pig tribe come wrap surround me with their rubbing and snorting. That mam knew but did not tell. Words of foulness creep between my hog teeth, they press for escape on the air. But I do not want them in Holly's space, these polluted sound shapes, and I clamp up my jaw to hold them within and they do rattle hard at my teeth.

'Maybe she was trying to protect you, Jack,' Holly says, but she does not believe of that. Her voice tells it.

I have to make some sounds or I will balloon with the holding. I tell that it is massive cruel, what mam did. Extreme cruel. I speak it in spitty words, the badness of telling that dad left on account of my hog head and my ugliness. Gulp breathing takes me and quakes me.

'I know, Jack, I know,' Holly soothes up. 'It was a disgusting thing to do. She was a nasty, heartless woman and she didn't deserve you.'

I let the gulping run out and I take my head into back times to dwell on one time past. It was after much whisky that mam talked of selling me, of passing me to circus ones. They were stopped at the crossing roads with their bright-lights and glitter rigouts. I watched in dark fall, from tree distance at the music and laughing, and way behind all that was the smell of beast fear and beast threat.

'You'll be a special attraction, Jack,' mam said with curly lips. 'Jack Plum, half man, half animal, the ugliest creature in the world.'

That fetched her laughing on and she swatted after me with the stick. She telled of huge whips what the circus ones would use to make me show myself and cages of metal to trundle me to busy roads as the humanbeast. I ran to Pardes Wood for full daytimes and I sleeped in with pigs at dark fall until the circus ones did go and mam was hungry and wetstinking and lashing.

My hog tongue comes over sour, the sick lumpiness rushes up at me and I dash upsteps to the sink so as not to taint the Palace. The spew is as yellow slime from pig birth and I heave it till my belly is in full ache and my skull also. And when I go back within the Palace, Holly and the pigtribe is in stillness for me.

'It is bad anger for mam what does fetch the vomits, Holly. The lying words, the blame thing she did make up on me and dad, not left, but in death and me not knowing. Was she still alive I would maybe kill her on account of it.'

Holly does make no reply but looks up on me with unhappy eyes, as she wants to give help but knows no way for it. And we do stare around within the silence as if we is trapped and the Palace is become a tomb place what gives no escaping from the outsideworld.

'I will now do it, Holly,' I tell, my deep angers at mam gives fuel to block my fear. 'I will start the butchering, this night, before dark fall outside-pig-run, and complete as it takes me all through nighttime, and pigtribe will eat and that which they do not will be fetched to Farmer Cotton's bins.'

'Maybe you should think about it for a while, Jack. You're upset now and you might regret it once you start because it's going be totally revolting. You know that, don't you?'

'It is only way, Holly, you did say that earlier time and it will let anger come out of me and stop frighteners entering.'

'I know I did, but I wasn't thinking straight then. There'll be blood everywhere and . . .'

'No,' I cuts in, 'no massive blood, not now. It will be as butchers chop and saw and slice. It will be extreme hard, Holly, in the stench, in the sight of it all, in the memory of what was but I must make it while my anger is full hot and it will give me extra strong ability. You must go out of here now, this is not for your eyes, ears or memory time.'

Holly stares with her full-of-life eyes to make me wonder what is to come from her now. 'We'll do it together, Jack,' she says. 'I'll help you.'

'No, Holly,' I say. 'You can not do this butchering. It will be much terrible stuff for your senses.'

'But I promised to protect you, to help you.'

'You did make full that promise, Holly, with the doctor phone stuff and the pension signs and the postalman and the percept of butchering and the uncovering of the Scrap-Book and the death of dad.'

'I think you need me here, Jack. Otherwise you could get overwhelmed with it all and it does have to be done before the maggots come, I know that for sure, and I know it'll be foul but I want to help.'

I know she has correct thoughts on the maggots and my overwhelming. It will be that space when the frighteners will try and take me fully. So we do splat hands and make the agreeing and that is when I know of a true friend, the one I will protect, in always.

'You is total sure?' I ask of her and she makes nods. 'Then we begin at it now as it will be long time doing. And your mam may get suspicions of things if you is much late.' Holly shakes her head.

'She's out, she won't be back until late. We've got time.'

Within the house we gather up old clothes, black dust-binday bags, dad's butchering tools and we make the preparations. Holly says we must have a ritual thing before the chopping. Some things what tell goodbye at mam and also goodbye at dad, as he is no more of warm blood and breathing air. We find some candles to help with that. We drag the blanketed body of mam upsteps to the backroom table for the butchering, to keep full sight from the Palace, and the pigtribe gather at downstep space, all of them, full tribing and Freya at lead space, all still, full with knowing of butcher things. Holly gets a bit of vomiting puke at the sink and she does look extreme faded. I tell that she may go from all this with no blame but she will not make to move.

'You need me here, Jack, I know you do,' she tells.

'Think only on the butcher thing, Holly,' I say. 'There will be no spurty bloods, dad telled me longtimes back on the chopping stuff. When they is dead some little while there is no gushing bloods. It will be like making the chumpy chops. But of stench, much will come.'

I give up to her pig muscles potion what has much eucalyptus within. 'Put the splodge under the nosespace and it does help. I see this at Blandish butchers.'

Then Holly and me is ready, dressed up in our rustling dustbinday bags and with candles lighted, and Holly's face the white of milk pudding as she makes a beginning of the ritual thing.

'This is a sacrifice we are making for the souls of Mr and Mrs Plum and to protect the soul still in the body of Jack Plum. We ask for help to make it all go easily and without too much splattering and smell,' she says, and then she does ask for the making of a pig song from my mouth after my words is made.

'May be you could have got happy if not for the hog I

was become, mam, but may be you could not and my horribleness is not full to blame for the poor thing you and dad did become to each and other. I can not forgive the terrible lies you telled on dad's departure, year up on year, making the blame on me. That is for your soul heart to live with in the beyond.'

'Amen,' Holly says.

'Amen,' I say and I give my throat a cough clearing before I sing:

> I saw a pig go flying by
> Heading for the Isle of Skye
> He smiled so sweetly, flew so neatly,
> I asked if I could have a try.
> Fly, flying over the sea
> A chunky pig piggy and me,
> Fly flying over the sea
> A chunky pig piggy and me.

'Will you keep singing while we do this?' Holly says and I do know it is for distraction of the horror what is up on us.

I tell I will try and we do look to the butchering charts what I found in among dad's tools what shows places to cut and saw and chop on pigs and cows and sheep. And from that we guess the where we should chop at mam's body.

'We don't have to take all her clothes off, do we?' Holly

says as I do make removals of mam's frock. And I understand full of that. I seen all of mam's flesh stuff because of the nappying and cleaning but it is not for Holly to do.

'No,' I tell, 'we can leave underpants and breast covers, Holly.' And this we do and I take up the pen markers to know of where to chop up on her lardy flesh. My hands does get quivery at this and Holly does close up her eyes tight. It is decided I do have the chopping job for my strong arms and Holly must do sawing and the cuts.

'When time comes, I will put saws and knife in at the places, Holly, so you may keep closed eyes while you do the cutting.' She does nod to me, still with tight shut eyes. Then we make a beginning and I give big breathing to drive reluctances off and I do soon know that Holly was correct in the possibility of my overwhelming. It does wave all up on me to run off within the woods, to take the pigs and Holly and run until feetsoreness does stop the escaping, to run and seek out Eden. In deep mind I know the outside-people would come and find and punish and lock away and only with Holly's presence do I have the strength and the purposefulness to keep up with the butchering. In this she was most right.

I do chop in sets of three – one, two, three – and it does help if I am full shouting then. As I am placing the blades of saw and knife upon the gashed flesh for Holly, I do sing as she did want. Within hogskull I tell myself I am at Blandish learning up on butchering. This is how we do keep at it even as it is total terrible. The stenching stinks; the splinter and cracking of bone what flies at every space; the wrenching off at shoulders, arms and legs; the cold, cold sweating up on my back and face. So much, I think me and Holly will faint full away or sick up great bilge stuff before we would come finished. The pigs stay extreme still and quiet below downsteps. They huddle, all herded up as I did guess it. Pigs do not like the butchering, it fears them of what stalks their lives.

After more than one hour I do stop, there is need of good air to breathe or my hoghead must burst wide open. Holly's eyes is still squashed tight and she does grip the knife in extreme tightness so that I must pull at each finger to fetch it free. All of her outside body is stiff but still shuddery within. The stink, the pulp, the bilge of it is total disgusting. And in my heart space is this turbulence of dad, all gone for ever, and foul thoughts on mam's vileness and lies.

'Do not look, Holly. We is stopping, to go within Palace for new water for our sawdust mouths and breathing air.' I wipe at my stickied up hand and take up Holly's titch one. 'I will take you to downsteps now. Okay?'

'Okay.' Her voice comes tight as stretched elastic.

At bottom of downsteps we do pause to take breath and Holly opens her eyes at me. They is filled of misery and tears, pictures and sounds what she will never lose. I do make a reminder to myself, that when we is done with this horror and I will tell how she can place those memories on back places within her brain space so they do not keep harming. And then sudden, in that comfort less stillness, we do hear of Samantha's voice in the above ground from us.

'Ho . . . lly! . . . Ho . . . lly!' she calls up and I have the fear she will bring humanpigadults up on us and I give up great gulpy sobs.

Holly does suck in at air and her eyes come starkish.

'I know you're here somewhere, Holly Lock!' Samantha calls again. 'Shall I tell your mam you creep out of the house in the dark? Shall I tell her you sometimes skip off school?'

Samantha's voice is filled of anger stuff and I have notice of hairs at my hoghead neck coming icy cold. Holly looks to me with total fear up on her and I think she must cry out loud in her dread of it all. I put up my gory finger at my lips for stillness. I have no solutioning at this point. It is too much to balance up in the hogbrain on the top of butchering and death. Holly takes a place behind my hog back, as she is hiding from what might come up on us, and as she does lean into me and grip at the dustbinday bags, they do crackle and rip within her hands and she does let some massive sobs burst out. Her titch body next mine is in full tremble as Samantha does call out an other time.

'I'll be watching you, Holly.'

Me, Holly and pigtribe wait downsteps for many panting breath times but there is no more to come of Samantha. I do sag as a wet sack on the scare of it and then I do turn and make notice of Holly holding at her breath with a blueness up on her lips. I lift her to my shoulders to rush the upsteps and at the sink she does get the choking, spluttering up spittle and slime. When I do let go of her for watering the sink out she slumps to the floor, her eyes total still and empty of life, as she is drifting off at an other far off place away from death and dread. Her titch hands is extreme cold and I do stroke and blow my warm breaths at them until she begins the fast canine pant what tells she comes back slow within real space.

Samantha's voice has fetched me full out to real time also, out from the rhythm of chopping and singing and pretending learning at Blandish butchers. And I do notice the gobby stains up on Holly, on face and arms, gory and lardy and below it, her own skin bleached out as cotton, and I lift her gentle to carry downsteps to pigcomforting. Her head does lollop side on side as a new born pig and I see of pearly sweat droplets on top her lips.

Up on the hay she lies full surrounded by the tribe who do snort low songs and nudge their sweet love at her and I do understand sharply as a knife plunge that I will do any thing what needs to keep her safe. When her eyes do have light in them I speak soft at her.

'Time for you to leave, Holly,' I say. 'Go change clothes and wash in the upstairs and discard bags there. I will finish what is to be done and clean all.'

'No, Jack, I said I'd help and I meant it.' There comes a throbby sound within her voice what I did not hear before, it makes a cold worry rush up on my back.

'Listen, Holly. You is extreme of courage but I should not have allowed this horribleness to come up on you. I give up my massive thanks as I did need you to stop the overwhelming of me, but I have overcome that now and you must go, please, and take much care of Samantha's skulking.'

Relief comes up on her and I do listen in full hush to her washup and clothes change upsteps with some of my hog ear up on the outsideworld and the possibility of Samantha's returning. I make full outside check for many minutes before Holly's leaving and notice how she is still in slight wobble when she departs. I wait on sight of her near by her own garden before returning below, where me and pigtribe sit in togetherness, to assist the gathering up of my strength, then I go to finish the awful butchering of mam's body. It does take much long time and I is in full raggedness come the end. Much time later, pigtribe eat all that is their ability without the pigdoor while within my hogskull is a clattering lamenting what edges desolation. On their return in to the Palace my legs splat out and I melt within hay like I might take shape as it.

It is like the hogbody does dissolve and become into floor and sawdust and hay, all mixed as one thing, not separated stuff but melded up in togetherness. I stay in that space and think on the 'what' that is inbetween all things, as air but not only that, as sun energy as well, and some other things what I have no words for that is not seen but is blobbing and battering all ways within all things. And now mam's body is within pigs and she is become sow as she did name dad, hog.

SIXTEEN

Holly Lock's world

Only just managed to get home without fainting. Something kept me going because I knew that if I did fall, I probably wouldn't be able to get up. My head was thudding, my legs were jelly, my stomach kept going into spasms like I might throw up again. It was late, everything was still except one lonely dog barking in the distance. My footsteps vibrated on the pavement, my head felt loose, my body was slightly out of time with everything else.

Dead bodies don't look that bad on TV, but they're revolting and the stink is the worst thing ever. I could still smell it on my hair and hands. All I wanted was to get in the shower, climb into bed, pull the covers over my head, have my stomach stop aching and my mind not replay the scene I'd just left over and over again.

I'd been out too early to see mam at breakfast, thank heavens, so I had no idea what mood she'd be in. A white car was parked in the drive. I had the presence of mind to feel the bonnet to see if it was warm. It was, so that meant they hadn't been back very long. After closing the front door very gently, I leant on it and listened because I was terrified that if she saw me she'd know something was wrong immediately. Her laughter filtered out of the front room. It sounded so ordinary, so cosy, so far away from dead flesh and bones it made me want to cry. Instead, the vomit decided it had waited long enough so I bolted for the downstairs toilet and retched until my stomach and throat felt like they were bleeding. Mam tapped on the door to see if I was all right, she wanted to know why I was throwing up. I imagined telling her and tried to visualise her reaction. I mean, how would you respond to something so revolting?

I told her I was fine and just wanted to be left alone, but she insisted I opened the door. When she saw how pale I was she offered aspirin and a hot drink. Somehow I didn't think an aspirin would do the trick. Shaking my head very slowly I let her know I just wanted to get to bed. She wasn't listening, again. She didn't even ask where I'd been, just tried to get me into the front room while she boiled the kettle but I shook my head. Why couldn't she see I was only just holding it all together?

When he called out her name, asking if everything was all right, the house suddenly felt unsafe. I slammed the toilet door but as the front room door clicked shut I let myself out and forced myself up the stairs. The first thing I did was get the shower running, then I threw everything I was wearing into my linen bin.

My brain went sort of haywire as I stood underneath the water. Fear, disgust, relief, all of them rippled through my tired body, fighting for attention. Then came the questions. Could they put me in prison for what I'd done? Was it actually a crime to chop up a dead body? Was Jack coping on his own? What would happen to him and me if we were found out? Would I end up in Durham prison?

My heart was pumping so fast I thought it might explode and vomit surged into my throat again but it was only slime and spit, there was nothing left in my stomach. My limbs were so weak I could barely dry myself and there still seemed to be a lingering scent of death around me. It was probably my imagination but I dabbed some of Samantha's perfume on my neck and wrists. It was horribly sweet but it took my mind off the other smell. Then I fell on to my bed and stared at the ceiling.

First my body went really hot, then immediately cold. It felt like everything was shutting down. My breathing became ragged and shallow as I sank into a dark, soundless space.

I woke up in Pardes Wood, walking with some of the pigs. Jack was in the distance by the river, waiting for us, but when I looked down at Freya, she had her own pig body but Mrs Plum's head and this long black tongue was sticking out of her mouth. I screamed and ran towards Jack, but he was sinking into the ground, like he was in quicksand. I woke up as mam came into the room and I grabbed hold of her so tight it must have hurt. She held me very close and rocked me a little, like she used to do when I was younger, and I was so relieved I began sobbing and talking at the same time.

'It was awful, mam, really awful.'

She made shushing sounds to comfort me and told me it was all right, it was just a dream and every atom in my body wished that was the truth. Mam's face looked so concerned and her arms around me felt so good, I opened my mouth to tell her the truth, that it wasn't a dream, that it was all horribly true, when this tall, fair-haired guy came into my room. He was wearing trackie bottoms but his chest was bare and really hairy. For some reason the sight of it made me want to scream again. To my horror he sat on the side of the bed and took hold of one of my hands. I leaned closer to mam and I could smell alcohol and stale tabs on her breath. 'Holly, this is Antony,' she said and he squeezed my hand gently. I pulled it away.

'It's okay, darling, it was just a dream, a silly dream.'

'It wasn't silly, it was fucking horrible!' I shouted.

When Antony said, 'D'you want to talk about it?' I shook my head. 'Maybe you'd like a glass of water?' he went on. I shook my head again. I didn't like him being so close to me, he smelt sour, a mixture of salt and sweat.

He nodded slowly and smiled at mam like they were sharing some secret.

'Go away,' I said, pulling the duvet over my head, and they

did, but before long I could hear them through the wall, talking softly together for ages. I was too scared to sleep. The numbness had gone but it had been replaced by restlessness. My head was full of sharp words and ugly sounds, which seemed to have a life of their own. At three-thirty I looked out of my bedroom window into the darkness and tried to imagine something soothing, but all I could conjure up was slime and bones and the uncomfortable sense of mam and Antony whispering in the next room.

In the morning I felt like I'd been through several cycles inside a washing machine. My body was full of jagged edges and something heavy seemed to be pressing down on my head. When I remembered I'd nearly blurted everything out to mam the night before, a hot tremor surged through me. I went downstairs in my dressing gown, desperate for a drink, and Antony was sitting at the breakfast table, reading a newspaper. A tiny lump of vomit rose into my throat, making me cough. I got myself a glass of water and headed for the door.

'Shall we try again, Holly?' mam called after me. 'This is Antony.' I ignored the hand he held out to me.

'Holly . . .' mam said.

'It's okay, Barbara,' Antony butted in, with a little shake of his head, which I wasn't supposed to notice. 'She's probably worrying about school.'

'No, I'm not,' I said. It was good focusing on Antony – feeling angry pushed the sick feeling away. I couldn't believe how comfortable he looked sitting at our table, in my chair.

I didn't want some guy wandering round our house, I'd never be able to relax. And those little shared glances, like I was the one who was in the way. I thought back to him walking into my bedroom, sitting on my bed, taking hold of my hand. It was outrageous. He was a stranger. It was one thing to go out with him, it was another thing altogether to give him free and total access to our home.

'So what is on your mind then?' he asked.

'That's my business.'

The doorbell rang and when I saw Samantha follow mam back into the kitchen I wished a hole would open up and swallow me. What with everything else, I'd forgotten about her shouting in Jack's garden the night before. Her eyes told me she hadn't. When mam introduced Antony she did her standing-on-one-leg-Barbie-Doll routine. It was all so unreal. Here I was in my own kitchen, where I should have been safe, but instead I felt surrounded by hostility and suspicion. I made a break for the door. The smell of the food was making me dizzy.

Samantha followed me upstairs. She was wearing that perfume she'd given me, and my belly started heaving again at the memory of trying to hide the death stench with it. I fell on the bed and tried to calm down.

'You're wearing the perfume I gave you,' Samantha said with a sense of triumph in her voice.

'It's crap,' I said.

'On you maybe,' she said. 'But then it would take more than perfume to turn you into a real girl.'

I tried appealing to her better side by telling her I was feeling weird about mam's new boyfriend being in the house. I said I was confused and not sure how to react, but I might as well have saved my breath.

'You don't get rid of me that easily. You owe me. I know you were out late last night and other nights,' she said, dropping the sugary smile. 'What were you doing, who were you with? Come on, tell me.'

'Fuck off, Samantha. I just want to be on my own.'

She ignored me and started slinking around my bedroom picking up my things and examining them, occasionally glancing at me with her know-all smile. I felt too weak to be bothered. Then she stopped by the bed and stared at me.

'You're shapeless, Holly, aren't you developing at all?' she said.

I pulled my dressing gown tight around me. 'At least I don't look like a child prostitute.'

Samantha laughed, she knew she'd hit a weak spot and was enjoying provoking me. 'No breasts, not even little pimples, no pubic hair . . .'

'Oh shut up, you sad cow, and stop staring at me.'

Grinning, she walked over to my chest of drawers and started looking through my underwear. 'Still wearing these high-up kid's knickers?' she said, holding some in the air. If

I'd felt stronger I would have kicked her to within an inch of her life. Instead, I tried ignoring her.

'You're very touchy today, aren't you? Maybe you're jealous of your mam's new boyfriend, he's quite cool, isn't he? And you've never had a boyfriend, have you? In fact, you've never even had a date. You're freaky and you dare call me sad.'

'Why the fuck can't you just leave me alone?'

'I feel sorry for you because you've got no friends and you look like a dog. And we've already got a secret, that *Chinese Horoscopes* book. So, I'm not going anywhere until you tell me what you get up to in Pardes Wood.'

Forcing myself to engage in conversation, I tried to side-track her. 'You wouldn't be interested.'

'Try me.'

'I look for rare plants, one in particular, an orchid.' I pointed at the chart on my bedroom wall, which showed drawings of unusual plants and where they'd been sighted. 'You can see them more easily at night.'

'You're joking!'

When I shook my head, she gave a short laugh, which sounded like a sheep coughing.

'That really is pathetic.' She walked over to my plant stand and shoved some of the pots irritably. I got off the bed and followed her. No matter how bad I felt, there was no way she was going to damage my plants.

I rubbed the leaves of the lemon geranium and held my

fingers up for her to smell. 'Isn't that amazing?' I said.

Samantha wrinkled her nose up. 'It's foul.'

'I always knew you had no taste, Samantha, and that proves it. Now bugger off.'

I went back to my bed and lay down with my back to her, hoping she'd finally go. Instead, she sat down next to me, and after a short while, put her hand on my arm and said my name very softly. When I turned, her face had lost its sulkiness and taken on a haunted expression. It was like she was remembering something she'd rather forget. She seemed younger as well, and more insecure than I'd ever seen her.

'Can I tell you something, Holly? Something really important and secret and just between you and me?'

The last thing I wanted was more secrets. I could barely cope with the ones I'd got. Rolling off the bed, I made for the door. 'No,' I said decisively, 'you can't. I don't want to know.' Opening the door wide, I lowered my voice. 'Now please go and leave me alone.'

She looked as if she was about to cry but I held my ground. 'You don't deserve a friend like me,' she said. For a moment I was struck by something in her voice, a sort of hopelessness, but it didn't last. You could never be certain when she was playing games.

She loomed over me at the door. 'Okay, Miss too-good-to-be-true,' she said, 'so how would you like me to tell your mam about you slipping out of the house after dark?'

'She wouldn't believe you.'

'Wouldn't she? Well, what if I told her I covered up for you about that book? The one with Jack Plum's dad's name in it?'

'Then she'd know you're a liar, wouldn't she?' Samantha wouldn't let go. She pointed her finger at me and moved so close that I could see one of her eyelids twitching.

'This has got something to do with Jack Plum, I know it,' she said. 'I don't believe all that garbage about plants. You might as well let me in on it, Holly, because I'm going to keep watch on you and the next time I know you're out in the dark I'll go straight to your mam. You've had your chance, no more warnings, right?'

The worst thing was I knew she meant it. Grabbing hold of her jacket I pushed her on to the landing. She was squealing like a baby when I slammed the door in her face and I heard her beginning to cry as she headed downstairs. Mam would no doubt give me an earful but at that moment I couldn't give a damn about anything except getting her out of my space.

SEVENTEEN

Troubles with Samantha

The pigs eat up extreme much of mam's body, as much as their ability, for the ritual and for me. The rest I hided amongst the dross and dribble of Farmer Cotton's bins which is taken away for destruction this next day time. It certain was a messy goodbye to this world for mam and I felt extra glad Holly was aside me for some of that time. She is brave and true of the heart. That absent soul smell within the butchering was full of dead times and foulness and I made the up windows well open the full day time. And I changed all hay in Paradise and watered down everything what was tainted.

There is still strangeness up on the house but the whisperings and cries are fainted away and a quietness is come, but in among it is feelings of more big worries about people in the outsideworld trying to get in at us. It says to me, this feeling, how they must discover about the death events, and me and Holly and the pigs, and then up they will come with shouts and hammers and their disgust full looks.

Those outsideworld people do always find things out. I have the thought in me to block the house entrance to the Palace. It is a growing thought. I have the electric down here and water so could fetch cooker and fridge. My clothes do by hand washing and I would get heat things down and bed so I live only within the Palace, that could become the safe way.

In dream time I see dad lots now, the ScrapBook pictures gave full reminder of all his face and body. My dream thoughts still dwell that he will come one day to fetch me to the after place with him. I sleep next dad's writing book and that maybe helps the dream times with him. I notice that dream and memory time of dad is with sun, always with shiny sun and patterns of shadows around.

This thinking on shadows gives the memory of time past when I did worry some at my own shadow, like it could be an unspeaking twin, what some time did hide and some time not, but ever was there. I have memory of naming that shadow and it was Nus, for the opposite way of sun. And when Nus was to be seen I made pretend with him of talk and song and the questions with answers and it was a brotherly sort of time. Best of it all was to talk of mam and her stick and bad words and Nus would be in sympathies. When dad went I never did speak at Nus again.

Holly is upset when she comes after the school. It is the death and butchering and the Samantha thing what is nipping at her. It is much burdens for her youngness and I have the wish of wanting to remove it all from up on her.

'I've been feeling really sick all day, Jack, how have you been?'

'Getting on with stuff, Holly, efforting to dwell up on other things, not smell and death. Fears of them fetching me for locking up is much great for me, worry of my pigs and you, that is greater also.'

'When I woke up this morning, just for the first few seconds, I thought I'd dreamt it all. And I remember now, all the time it was actually happening, I was in a sort of daze, set back a bit, like I was watching myself instead of being myself. Does that make any sense?'

'Yes, Holly, yes, it's there in the brain core text, that way of side slipping. It's like protection stuff, so horrible things can be dealt with. Humanpig brains is clever things. And you did this all for me and for pigs and that is so extra brave. It was not for you, it was for us and I am full grateful and full admiring of the courage.'

'Did the pigs . . .?'

'It is all done and completed, Holly, and in our past times now. You must put the pictures and smells and sounds of it all on to a shelf far off back within the brain.'

'How can I do that?'

I make explanation to her on how to think on the brain as if it lives within a big room what has much cupboards and shelvings and boxes. And the job is to make selection of one box, or shelf, in a far place, to put away all worrying thoughts or remembrances. Then a memory label is stuck on this place, that it is of past times, and only to be opened up when it is of special choice.

This talk did seem of some help and Holly did lie with Peach for cuddles up on the new hay. She stared into herself for some time and gave up small sighs and then once did make more vomit into the nearby bucket. I cleaned it all away and opened up pigdoor for some minutes of true air. Then Holly closed her eyes and got rested. I did wipe the hot head with clean towels and water and watch of her stirrings and snufflings just like a piggylet. And later Peach did lick at her neck in softness and comfort and Holly waked some little way better. I gave her water for flushing out the stomach.

'Samantha's like a flaming bloodhound, Jack,' she said then. 'She sniffs around everywhere, she's really doing my head in. What can we do? She won't stop until she thinks she knows what I'm up to and I don't ever want her to come into the Palace. It would be ruined if she came. What can we do, Jack? We have to do something.'

It makes pain to see Holly as this and so I torture my hogskull to dig out solutions stuff. Because she has done planning things for me and I want to give back some same things. And it comes into me slow and it talks almost in replica of dad's voice, one possible way. And when I tell Holly I have the idea, her face stops the creasing and takes up hope full.

'What is it?' she asks.

'It is of the outside nighttime wanderings,' I say. 'You might fetch Samantha to the pigs in their plodging time and maybe she will ride up on Freya. She is not piggirl as you, so she could come fed up soonest and then stop the pestering of you. Would that be a satisfactory to her?'

'I'm sure it would, but I don't want her anywhere near the pigs. You don't understand what she can be like.'

Some frightsigns up on my neck do tell me that Holly may be in correctness but no other solutioning will come at me. I ask if Samantha will do the watching and follow as she did make threat.

'I wouldn't put anything past her, Jack, she likes getting her own way and she can't bear the fact that I'm involved in something which she's excluded from.'

I make explanation to Holly that we will get extra danger if Samantha makes discovery of the Palace in her watchings. If she does observe at all times it could come possible for her to see Holly on visitings and then she will know of the entry within the garden and this would bring terrible dangers. Then I tell that the fetching of Samantha to nighttrotting time could become the way for protecting the Palace, may be. So that if we do give her the one thing, what is nighttime trottings, she may be would not do the regular watchings. Holly thinks on this for much time and I do notice the twists and turns of her eyes and mouth until she reaches the time to speak.

'Would you do that, Jack? Let her ride Freya? It's such a special thing to give to someone and Samantha just doesn't deserve it.'

I let Holly know it is not given up to Samantha, but for Holly, and that makes the working of it. So we do give and we do get back, but she does still makes looks of uncertainness and I do have to say we has not much choices. Samantha must be stopped of her dangerous watchings and I cannot think on an other solution. I throws it to Holly, that if we do not offer pigriding, then she does have to find suggestions. After some long thoughts and pacings on thisthat way possibilities, she makes agreement on it, even though not her or me are full content.

'I'll have to be cool about it, tell her it's a special secret which she has to promise to keep to herself. She'll be really pleased about that.'

Some dusk leaves Holly's face with this. It has done some settling of her agitations and after some sighs she does ask if we can make the Samantha offer for this nighttime, which I do make agreement on. Then I give up dad's writing book to her and ask for the reading to make ease on us both and she is pleasure full to do it. We sit atop the hay with my eyes closed for the listening.

'He hasn't written that much, Jack,' she says and the goldy-edged pages do swish at her beginning.

I nod to her without the opening of eyes. I am seeing dad glancing back to me from long times back, and he grips the special pen. It is a good look he is giving, a knowing. And then Holly is at it.

She's getting through three bottles of whisky a week now. Got in from work the other day and found she'd hit Jack so hard with that damned stick of hers, that all his fingers were swollen. Burnt the stick in the garden.

These words give up a lumpiness in the throat and Holly notices my catchy breathing and asks if she should stop, but I tell her I do want more.

Jack loves me reading to him now. He's got this fascination with Piglet in the Winnie the Pooh stories, especially all the big adventures they have. He's even learnt some new words.

Holly makes smiles at me as she turns over the page. She does enjoy this telling of dads.

After dinner tonight – which is usually her best time – brought up the idea of sending Jack to school. Pointless. Just got a load of abuse.

I stop Holly then. I do not enjoy the misery of dad's words and the picture of me as that small thing and dad being full of upset and help less. I ask for her to search on to less glum things written and she does.

Had to get out of the house tonight. Her voice was driving me mad. Took Jack to see Farmer Cotton's new pig litters. He loved them. Bizarre how the mother sows let him get close. Terrified they'd bite him but they didn't. Couldn't sleep again. Felt like me and Jack are trapped.

Early morning. Took Jack to the farm again. Sat him on a Tamworth sow. Amazing. Totally at ease.

Holly stops the reading there and looks a question at me and makes a point at my pigs.

'Are these all Tamworth pigs, then?'

'Nearly,' I say. 'They is red and prick-eared and they are not many within this land, dad told me, that's some more reason why my pigs is special. Others is named cross breeds, with the Large Whites. Look, see that bristle hair colour, can be lightest of ginger, to chestnut to dark red. Is beautiful hair, just like Holly's.'

'I hate having red hair.'

'Oh no, you must like, Holly, you is rare.'

Holly smiles. I see she enjoys what I say so I tell more, like Tamworth does have longer snout from other piggies and Freya does snort to show and gives one great nudge at Holly and she smiles more.

I tell her to read more and I do close my eyes to find dad's face. I hear Holly turn pages some more times before reading.

Plans well advanced now. Me and Jack started digging out the cellar. Hard work but he's tireless.

Holly stops to tell only one page of dad's writing is left. I do not want the end of it, these pictures of him and me together.

Jack's really confident now. Goes to the farm on his own. Thinks the pigs understand his chatter. Pig Palace going well. Started the tunnel into Pardes Wood yesterday. Off to the city tomorrow, need some more books on breeding.

Holly makes a stop again. She closes up the diaries and stares into the ground.

'That's it, Jack,' she says extra quiet, 'that's the last thing that's written.'

I nod. I can not make good words, my clotted up throat will not allow and snot runs as water. Holly gives a T-shirt at me from her sporty bag for the messiness to be wiped. I have sorrowfulness in my hoghead, but is glad also from hearing new things of dad, good times, just as memory and dream time did tell.

'Was that end time, Holly . . . before death?' I ask.

Holly nods extreme slow. 'Yes, I think so, Jack. The death certificate date is for the next day. Are you all right?'

I pretend okay.

I am not much for talk just now and we agree the meeting time for Pardes Wood and outside plodging and the bringing of Samantha. Aftertimes, when Holly is gone, I lie full on the hay and make some extra crying stuff and the pigs rock in gentle ways with soft snorting. I remember back on all times I can conjure of me with dad and I know I had especial times and an extreme good dad what showed me things on pigs and digging and building and telling time and some words and gave me extra deep loving. Now mam is departed I think on the 'ifs'. If dad had stayed living, if I had gone schooling, every if I can provoke from memory. But, far in depths of my hogbrain core text I absorb that 'if' is as nothing, as cobweb and as unpossible dreams. Mam did live in the 'if' place and that was like jail for her, so I will not take that into me. It is well to dwell in the inspiring things some times, and it is well to have planning but not to live in past places where you could get horrible stuck.

To fetch resting I think in on piglegends for calming. It is said of Quinling, what made first humanpig bonding, longtime back, maybe he had not, then pigs would not get butchered. The reckoning of this was, coming full aware of pig cleverness, humankind did have reason to slaughter. This is as some tribe persons did, to eat of their strong enemy people and take within their strengths. And, it is also reasoned, to keep pigs in a down place, cast away of no acknowledgement. The humanpig does have a need to be topmost of all creatures and will consume up in various many ways any that make challenge. But, it be true legend or not, Quinling did make his bond with the monkman and we can not go back from those eventings.

EIGHTEEN

Holly Lock's world

Samantha was hanging out with Colin as I approached my gate but she strolled towards me, leaving him on his own. I noticed how he adjusted the way he was standing so he looked taller and wondered what sort of strange snakes lived in his brain.

As usual Samantha came too close. It was like she had no idea about personal space. Mrs Dove had done stuff about it in class, got us all to stand up and turn around, with our arms stretched out, to show what she meant. Samantha was sulky and itching for trouble. My first impulse was to shove her back a bit – instead, I took a step sideways. Before she could start on me I told her about the secret I was going to share with her. Not what it was, just when and where she had to meet me, midnight at the entrance to Pardes Wood. Her expression changed to pleasure.

I looked beyond her towards Colin. 'Swear you won't tell anyone about this, either before or after, or the deal's off.'

'I swear on my dad and mam's life,' she said before squeezing my hand. Colin pretended not to be watching but I knew he was.

'Make sure he doesn't get too curious,' I told her.

She smiled and winked at me. 'I'll tell him it's girl's stuff, he's not interested in that.'

Mam was making tea when I got home. When I told her I wasn't hungry, there was one of those loaded silences while her face went slightly red.

'You're just trying to punish me because Antony's started staying over, aren't you?'

God, how did we get from there to here, I thought? 'No,' I replied, 'I just don't want anything to eat. And while we're talking about it, I'm going to become a veggie as well, so I don't want any more meat.'

'This is ridiculous! I know that look, you're trying to make me feel guilty?'

She obviously did feel guilty so I said nothing, just got myself a glass of water. My head was still full of strange sounds and thoughts and the feeling that someone was watching me, ready to pounce. Come to think of it, that was probably guilt. Also, I was fed up that Samantha was going to get to ride Freya when she didn't deserve it. Far from getting to ride a pig, she needed to learn how to leave people alone.

'Anyway, what about our quiz?' I said, when I was fed up of the silence and the heavy stares.

'Not tonight,' she said, tight-lipped.

'Why not?' I wanted my proper routine back. So many things outside the house were horrible and confusing, why did my life at home have to fall apart as well?

'Antony . . .' she began.

Enough said. I started to walk past her when she grabbed at me, scraping my arm with her nails. It wouldn't have happened if I hadn't been feeling so upset, but the pain just floored me for a few seconds and I lashed out.

'For fuck's sake!' I said as I pushed her away. 'Just leave me alone.' That's when I got a slap across my face. I couldn't believe it at first. The room seemed to dip and swerve and I thought I was going to pass out but mam was so angry she didn't even seem to notice.

'How dare you use that language to me!' she yelled. 'Get to your room and stay there, you can do without anything to eat tonight and you can stay there till morning.'

'You wanted an argument, didn't you? You want me out of the way, shut in my room, so I don't get in the way when he comes round.'

I closed the door before the plate in mam's hand smashed against it. In my room, I struggled to barricade the door with my chest of drawers and pushed the top end of my bed up against the chest and the bottom against the wall. Then I fell on the bed and started sobbing quietly.

'If you come out of there before morning you'll be grounded for a week,' she shouted from the landing.

Things were really out of hand. Nobody teaches you about death or dads running off or mams getting boyfriends. They just think you need maths and English. My insides seemed to be tied up with elastic bands and I felt so angry all the time, except when I was with Jack and the pigs. It wasn't fair that Samantha was going to meet them and get to ride Freya and it wasn't fair that mam was more interested in Antony than in me. How did it all get so messed up?

I lay on the bed trying to get a grip on my anger. I wanted to kick things, smash stuff, anything to make me feel better. I thought about my dad, about why he left, and I thought about Jack's dad, and how he must have felt when he realised he was going to die and wouldn't be there to care for his unusual son. I think people do that, when they're about to pop off, I think loads of stuff zings through their brain, stuff they wish they could do something about. I wish I'd had a dad like Jack's, instead of a waster who ran off smelling of oil and fags.

No amount of lying about was going to make things any better, though. I needed to do something positive. After checking all my plants, I rubbed the lemon geranium leaves and breathed the scent in deeply. The fruity fragrance was both soothing and energising. It made me realise that some good things had come out of all the horror. Mrs Plum's body was gone, Jack was safe for the moment and we were dealing with Samantha.

The best thing to do was get some rest. Setting my watch alarm for eleven-thirty, I closed my aching eyes and tried taking Jack's advice, about seeing the brain as if it was in a room. I put all thoughts of Mrs Plum's death and disposal into the far dimness at the distant corner, inside a white box.

NINETEEN

The outside time

Me and pigs wait on wood's threshold spot for Holly to fetch Samantha. This is the beginning of leaf and branch blocking sky in great fullness. It is tree and earth domain and I have discovered in past times their vast patience in respect of plunderers. Still, in contra to that toleration they some times do splat out smells and barbs and soft earth and plunging holes at invaders who dis respect. I shut my lids and listen in to their blibberings and know they are not restful and this gives me a small, bleak chill as they is usual welcoming of pig tribe and me. I have my first impulsing that I am wrong in the bringing of this Samantha.

I catch the Holly scent in my hog nostrils before the seeing of her, as does the pigs. Peach runs for the scenting, us waits in apprehensions. I telled the pigs before of the intruder, Samantha, who is to come and they will do a co-operate without any liking of it. Even now they is in instinct of my new waverings they will proceed as my desires be.

Samantha links her arm up to catch hold on Holly and when they come at us in the dark silence I notice some streaky fear along her eyes. But she has bold stuff, I sense this, and she has been much fear full before times. In closeness I apprehend her big damage and my regretfulness grows until I must slap it back or let the frighteners take a hold. Her legs is not protected of trousers and her clothes is extreme bright what sticks out loud in this greenery place.

'This is Jack Plum,' Holly says with crossness.

'I know this is Jack Plum,' Samantha says. 'I've seen him loads of times.'

'A . . . aa . . . and . . . ddd did ll . . . ll . . . laugh at mmm . . . me,' I say. She is much surprised by this out loud voice, which is behaving good for Holly. I give out my hand as is proper. 'H . . . h . . . hello S . . . S . . . Sam . . . antha,' I say as I think it will be best to make a peace thing among these girlpigs.

She thinks some few seconds before reaching her hand at me and Holly stays tight of anger, then Samantha makes the handshake.

'Hello, Jack Plum,' she says with eyes dropping back to the usual way of wariness. 'So, it's all about pigs, eh?' she says. Her voice tells she does not believe this as truth.

The pigs stay in extreme stillness, only snuffling close, except of Peach who leaps to be in Holly's region. Holly bends for strokes and cuddling and Samantha comes by one side of me. There is a shape in her face, far back behind the eyes what is a reminder of mam, something mangled.

'Well then?' she says. 'Is this it? Do we just stand around here all night?' And when she laughs it is of a glass crackling.

'What is your extreme pestering of Holly all for, Samantha?' I ask.

She looks to me with a twisty, hurted mouth. 'I don't pester her, I'm her friend, her only friend. And if everybody finds out she's been with you, she'll never have any more friends.'

Her words do come up sideways. She moves in on too much space of me and I make steps away but she does like a shadow, keep up extreme close. This too closeness of her shows me the wasted upness within her, it is stinging to my soulheart.

Within Freya's sideswaying I see of worryings. She has the duty of her sounder, they look at her for judgements. I give her my touch for assuring and signal the time for the romping and mudlarking. We set ourselves off in to the deep of the woods at a quickness.

On the shelves inmost my hog skull stir things extra cautious. Tremble things what are for warning. This is due from Samantha's mangled parts what is far back and will not be approachable from pig sweetness as it does not take comforting. There sits the danger what Freya and I know, almost like it might be touched, and now there is no way into the past time before Samantha, it is done and we will have the consequence.

Pardes Wood looks on at us, all intruders but some known and usually welcomed in. A tree branch snares to Samantha's clothing, plucks with unfriending, brackens do scratch at her legs and she makes a jangling screech.

'Oh no, look at my bloody cardigan!' she calls. 'I hate this wood, can't we go somewhere else?'

'No,' Holly snaps.

And I get awareness that this is what the trees have knowledged, Samantha's dis ease for them, and they will spite and crush if they do mind to, so I get a relief flush when the river is reached and the tree crowding is less.

Soon Samantha questions about the pig riding what Holly has telled and I call up on Freya for this task as previously agreed with her, my main pig.

Freya drops her rear end low for Samantha to clamber up, then does sway off extra slow as telled. But the girlpig calls out unsatisfied with the slow and does yell for more.

'Faster! Faster!' she calls. 'Come on, whoopee! Faster! Look at me, Holly! Look at me!'

Holly's face stays within a shadow, much heavy, as sky before full rain. She keeps up the staring and the biting into her lips until soon she wants of no more. 'Stop her, Jack,' she says, 'stop her, she'll wear poor Freya out.'

'It will be well, Holly. Freya will stop when ready . . . watch . . . Freya gets the angers now.'

Samantha will not end the shouting demands for faster

and she even starts at slapping on Freya's haunch. Freya looks to me and I give her the nodding as agreed before time and she runs extreme fast then does stop as sudden so Samantha flies from the pigback with shrieking and dumps heavily on mudgrass.

She does look as a sad piggylet, one what is not loved by her mamsow. I want Holly to make notice on this wounded up piggirl but she is much angered up on Samantha's pigriding.

'Help me up, Holly?' she does say, for her feet do slide up on the scummy ground. But Holly will not give up assistance. I do not want Samantha's raging to come up on my tribe so I make a lift of her to the grassy banking.

'Thank you, Jack,' she says, 'you're very kind, and very strong.' Then she gives up what Holly calls as one of her pukey giggles. But it is not of laughter stuff, it is of despairing.

'Time for you to go now, Samantha,' Holly says. 'That was the deal.'

The pigs get into the ending of the wallow plodging and wait quiet for what is next. There is some atmosphere of the bad energy and the trees seem to claw in towards us. I notice the bird song has paused up as well and I full regret one more time the coming of Samantha.

'But I want to see where the pigs live. Jack won't mind, will you?' Samantha stares to me with the pleading look and she presses in to closeness at me. I have confusion at her coldness within warmth skin. Her hand touches at mine and she makes a finger stroke up on the palm spot.

'No!' Holly shouts, in full sharpness.

'But that's not fair. I want to come with you and Jack.'

A rushing train belts past the extreme of the wood heading for the farlands and I gather the time is now late. My pigs have need of feed and sleep and peace fullness.

'This little piggy . . .' Samantha says alongside a little smile and an even littler voice and she does the stroke thing at my hand again. My hoghead does get heated up with Samantha's changefulness, one time fear full, then at her games. Her inside confusion trickles out up on everything.

'This little piggy . . .' she says again as she moves full close on to me, side on side.

'That's enough!' Holly shouts. 'Jack, you wait till me and her have gone, then you take the pigs to home, okay?'

I nod and Samantha is full of moans. 'Come on, you,' Holly tells her.

'No, I want to go with Jack and you. I don't want to go home.' She moves so in to me I feel her breaths up on my arm and she throws whispers up to my big hoghead.

'What are you whispering?' Holly says.

'That's between Jack and me.'

'She says . . .' I begin and Samantha's groans shake her small head but Holly is my true friend who I can not ever let down. These two is in hot conflicting of each other but there is the friend thing in back of it all but not getting out, so I do speak it even as I do fear of consequences. 'She says she will give show of her arse to me if –' Holly does not want the finish of all the words and she takes the hold on Samantha's arm.

'You're fucking disgusting,' Holly shouts. 'How would you like it if I told your mam and dad what you just said?' Then she tries to drag the girlpig off from me but Samantha makes the big struggle.

'I don't care what you do,' she screams.

'Right then, let's go and tell them.'

'Your mam'll kill you if she finds out you've been with Jack Plum.'

I know this to be truth even before I glance on Holly's whitesheet face. I do not like the 'kill' word made in near-by of the pigs so I back off away and gather the pigs towards me for departure. Holly has a dragging hold on Samantha.

'No, Holly, don't!' she cries, 'please . . . I don't want to go home . . .'

Her voice comes full of pain and leaks from the snarled place within her and I feel a confused mood for her hurt but also for Holly and the pigs' need and I struggle with this question of tendering to both. They battle at hands and kicks for some while before Samantha gets freedom to run.

She scrambles through the dark layering trees and they lash at her and push obstacles at her path and I have worries of her reaching the end of Pardes Wood in safeness. I make attempt to tell Holly of how Samantha has some breakages inside but she is much filled up with anger and will not hear my words.

'Don't take any notice of Samantha,' she says of her serious voice. 'I've told you, she cries all the time to make people do what she wants. Some people are like that, Jack, they always try and use you.'

I want Holly to know what I can pick out, what I have discovered from time with the pigs. That hurt is shown for some reasons, that it is there to find comfort before it must go extra sour and into danger.

'She's not hurt, Jack,' Holly insists. 'She's cross because she can't get her own way, that's different.'

But I think it is not so. All of them, cross, angry, shouty, fighty, all of them are come from hurt, unless you is foulpig or foulhumankind which is wicked from circumstances of birth which Samantha is not.

'We will make to follow, Holly, so we see her get free of wood, this is my wish.'

Holly is full of reluctances but she has sense of my determined plan and this is the thing we do.

And all the walk back time, Freya and the pigs is extreme reserved, within their tribe, separate out from me and Holly and giving up dread feelings. I am not full protecting them from humanpigs, as is necessary, and I must not fetch more troubles at them or up on the world of Holly. She can not be known as 'Freak friend' to outsideworld people. This would stumble her growing.

My self wishings should not be more than safeness to Freya and tribe and Holly Lock. Maybe the horrors of mam, her death, the butchering, did bring some gash within the Palace, some entry for frighteners and outsidepeople to get access. If this is happened I must make repairs, find the ways of extra protecting. There is ways of ensurement and I will contemplate on the Boar star of this night for knowings. Boar star what understands from wayback pig and humantimes pathways what was taken for good and not for good. And I do ask I will get the guiding, especial if it is done at pigrelicstone.

TWENTY

Holly's Lock's world

I got up the trellis and back into my bedroom unnoticed, only to hear sounds of Antony and mam filtering through the wall. For one small moment I thought they were redecorating her bedroom, then the mist cleared. They were having sex. Obviously they didn't care whether I heard or not. Why couldn't they go and do it at his house for a change? I put a CD on loud to drown the noise, ran a bath, soaked in the tangerine suds and made a promise to myself that if I ever had children of my own, I would never treat them shabbily, the way mam was with me. The lumpy knot in my stomach was still nagging at me and I wondered if it would ever go away. It was like I was hungry but stuffed at the same time and I was so angry when I thought about Samantha.

What the fuck was wrong with her? Pressing herself against Jack and stroking his hands like that. I could tell he didn't understand what she was up to but I did, wearing that short skirt and cropped top to show her belly-button piercing. She was trying to flirt with him, trying to get him to do what she wanted.

I don't think Jack's got much idea about sex and I'm certainly no expert. I've had a few snogs, which weren't up to much, especially with their bloody tongues down my throat making me gag.

What goes on in Samantha's stupid head? Jack was actually worried about her, and expected me to sympathise. No way. We should never have let her in on our secret. My whole body flashed cold at the thought of what she'd do next.

The problem was in Jack being clever and yet innocent as well. He thinks if he can see hurt in someone they should be treated gently. He doesn't understand someone like Samantha because he's had so little experience. I've seen what she can do if she thinks she's been thwarted. I've seen her lash out and it's not nice and she can change without warning. One minute she can be all over someone and the next, it's as if they don't exist.

Half an hour later, I woke up in the cold bathwater, shivering. The noises from the next room had stopped, thank God, so I put my pyjamas and dressing gown on, pulled the bed away from the door and crept down to the kitchen. What I needed was a hot drink to warm me up and something bland to eat to help settle my stomach.

Putting the kettle on to make some of mam's camomile tea – she always has it when she's got a headache – I stuck two slices of bread in the toaster. The sink was full of dirty dishes. Mam's habits were changing. A week ago she wouldn't have dreamt of going to bed without washing up. I checked the lounge out while the toast cooked. Antony's shoes and socks were lying on the carpet like some symbol of ownership, of him taking over our space. There was an empty bottle of wine and the remainder of a couple of joints in an ashtray. They'd been smoking dope.

'Bastard,' I said out loud because it sounded good.

'Who, me?' Antony said from behind.

My heart rushed into my throat as I realised he'd come downstairs after me. I turned to face him ready for a confrontation. He was wearing mam's bright pink dressing gown and it was bulging open around his hairy chest. Why couldn't he wear something more appropriate?

'If the cap fits,' I said, determined not to let him intimidate me.

In the kitchen behind him, the bread in the toaster jumped up. I took it as my cue to get out of the lounge. As I got level with him, he moved in front of me and for the first time I felt a wisp of fear. For all I knew he could be a pervert. I stepped back and away from him and I think he realised what I was thinking. He put his hands up in a conciliatory gesture.

'I'm sorry, Holly, I didn't mean to frighten you,' he said.

'You didn't,' I replied.

He followed me into the kitchen but kept some distance

between us. He didn't say a word, just watched me as I buttered my toast and made the tea. I put it all on a tray as he began what I guessed was a prepared speech.

'I'm not trying to come between you and your mam, Holly,' he said, 'I'd like us all to get on, if that's possible. Barbara's miserable when you're upset and that doesn't help any of us.'

'She didn't sound very miserable a short while ago.'

He opened his mouth to speak again but changed his mind when I turned away from him and headed for my bedroom. The toast tasted delicious and the tea was bearable but getting one over on Antony felt even better. My stomach settled down, but later, when I tried to sleep, I got flashbacks of Mrs Plum's body, of things I'd seen the few times I'd opened my eyes. The bulging veins on her legs; the thick, curled-up toenails; one leg, separated from the body, thumping on to the floor. And the disgusting sound of that chopper cracking through bone and muscle.

It was only by repeating to myself, it would all turn out okay and I'd done it for the right reasons, that I was able to relax at all. Hopefully Samantha would soon get bored with being on my case, as I couldn't see her getting interested in breeding pigs, and Jack certainly wasn't what she expected. On the other hand, I'd seen her in action before, causing trouble. She was relentless. Mrs Dove once said, 'Samantha, you've got no thermostat!' And I knew what she meant. Samantha doesn't know when to stop and you can't trust people like that because they hurt you and they don't even realise they're doing it.

To comfort myself I got my pad and flower books out and started drawing a design for an ideal garden, the sort I wanted to have when I got my own place. Lots of border perennials, some rockery perennials and then other plants which would change with the seasons. Drawing shapes for borders, I made lists of potential plants and marks for trees and water features. My first list included columbine (*aquilegia bertolonii*), campion (*lychnis coronaria*), feverfew (*tanacetum parthenium* 'Snow Puffs') and goat's rue (*galega orientalis*).

I said the Latin names out loud, over and over again – the sound was gentle, soothing, optimistic. I named wild plants that would look good amongst the trees and which I could seed from Pardes Wood: wood garlic (*allium ursinum*), meadowsweet (*filipendula ulmaria*) and honeysuckle (*lonicera periclymenum*). My eyes closed with the scent of fresh grass circling my brain.

TWENTY-ONE

Respite in the Palace

I made some beginning in the sealing of the inhouse entrance to the Palace within the dawning hours. It is to be completed right and good so no clue is remaindered and is a big task. I carried all I have need of, fridge and stuffs, to the Palace, using my wheelie trolley with fat boards covering the down steps. Time come I will make visit to new housebuildings they make back beyond the Mrs Robson shop, for plaster things, wood and such.

Farmer Cotton got donated two new girlpiggylets for his especial breeding pod this bright morning time. Nodger knows they are come from him and Freya and he will give protecting. Earliest morning times, in the dewglistening fields, I forget the problems of me and the outsideworld people. Everything looks like the world can be good, animal and humanpig and monsters all in it together. That mood thing does not last to real morningtime, when noise full, angry cars line up on the roads and the raging inside them gets more and more. And they blow the fagend smoke from windows and tap tap up on the steerwheel and some times they shout and pappappap horn sounds. They become consumed with fuss.

I try to put the frightchill of Samantha away from my head. She is so much of the outside, so much of the hurt of the outside that I fathom danger. Holly will be full protected in all this, I will do it with no restriction on necessaries.

I made a treat for Holly in the last of the dark time. A thing for her to dwell up on. And here she does come with the flute and the smile, fetching her specialness within the Palace. She does not notice my treat at firstly, because the pigs wrap surround for flute time and swaying. After the tunes for them to snuffle and shuffle at she plays 'Catch the Wind' for me to have pleasure. Her eyes get brimmed up with questions when she looks full to me.

'What?' I ask.

'He's been there again, that Antony,' she says. 'I'll hate it if he moves in, Jack, I really will.'

I make questions of her on what she hates in this Antony and I get understanding that it is not this man but any man what took her mam's love would not come welcomed. And I sense that she will get knowing of this before much long time so I do soothing.

'It might not come to happening,' I tell her, because things do not all ways.

'But what if it does? I couldn't come and live here, could I?'

I feel some thrills at her want in coming to me, it signals the truth of the friend thing and I can not make a recall now of the living with Holly not in it. But I have to make sense answers to her, not the unwise wishing kind.

'The outsideworld people would not like, Holly, and they do have the grip on the world and all its force and fury.'

'Couldn't we run away, Jack? Go to a new place with the pigs, somewhere a long way from the outside world? Maybe to Eden, where your dad came from?'

When she says these fantasy thoughts I understand she is still so much of young and I am part of grownup. I have learned the full suspiciousness of the outsideworld on more than several times and she knows only some little.

'Not in possibility,' I say. 'We have none of money, of house to stay at, of land, of car or van, and all outside-worldpeople would come against us, searching to find us, to lock-me-up-and-throw-away-key.'

'It's crap, this world,' Holly says in her downlow mood.

She does not want to talk more so she leans backward up on the hay for rest of her thoughtbulging head and she sees the treat of my doings. I painted the patterns of stars up on the sky the last dark time on the bilberryblue of the Palace ceiling space.

'Oh Jack, how did you do that?' she asks with wonder layered in her voice.

'Lie outside, look, make remembrance, come in and paint. Easy,' I say, tingling up.

'It's not easy, Jack, really. You must have a great memory.'

'Yes, look . . . Orion . . . Rigel . . . Sagittarius. Dad showed, brought books of star sky pictures, and learned me of them. I like the dark time, not see the Freak then.'

'You're not a Freak, Jack.'

'You see . . . inside . . . not just . . . Freak body.'

We take notice of my stars for some long while and Holly plays extra flute tunes and it is like dreamingtime – special – and the pigs feel this also. The dangers from the outsideworld seems to get more little on this time and that is good.

'You all right, Jack . . . really? Y'know, after doing your mam's body and Samantha and all?' Holly asks after some silent space.

'Yes . . .' I say, but with caution on the sounds.

'We did it, though, Jack. We stopped them taking you away, didn't we?' I nod to let her words come on. 'I can probably cope with Antony if I have to,' she says. 'I'll just keep out of the way but I don't want Samantha spoiling it all by blabbing.'

'She was within the gardenspace and at the house door this morning time,' I tell Holly. I was to keep it away of her but I see she is in need of truth.

'She came right up to the house?' Holly says and I nod. 'You didn't speak to her or let her in, did you, Jack?'

There is the frights coming up on Holly's eyes. 'No!' I say. 'No, I used the mam's voice: "Go away, horrible child!"'

'That's good, let's hope that scares her.'

'May be, Holly, but she is in . . . much needing.'

'She's a mess.'

'She walks in . . . in . . . shadow places.'

'Something like that,' Holly says not with full convincing. 'I've been thinking, Jack,' she goes more serious. 'What we did with your mam, we had to do it, to save you and the pigs, okay? But now . . . we have to somehow forget it . . . put it behind us. Don't you think so?'

'As I did say, on backmost shelves in brainspace. Past times.' And we put attention at my stars some more.

'Samantha might come to Pardes Wood again, on her own,' Holly says, extreme quiet and without a look to me, and I know it to be true from the tremoring of my throat. 'You should change the times you go, Jack. A different time every night and a later time, so that she doesn't catch you. She'll get fed up eventually.'

'I will do. But can you not come any more times, because of that? The pigs and me will come to miss you at them times.'

Holly thinks for some while to make the plans. 'I'll come on Music Club nights,' she tells. 'Samantha comes to the club and then I'll walk home with her and go to my house. Then later I'll come and meet you. We'll agree a time, okay?'

I nod okay but she is not full finished.

'Jack?' she questions.

I wait in wondering at what is next to come.

'D'you like Samantha?'

'She is not easy for liking on account of her damages.'

'But she is pretty and sort of grown up, in her body I mean.'

'Not pretty within.' I have no guess what Holly is examining in this.

'But when she said, y'know, about showing you her . . . her . . .'

'Arse?'

'Yeah, I mean, what did you think?'

'Didn't think, you telled of her to shut up and hoghead went thinking on to that.'

Holly does the sighing thing then and gets over fidgetting so it has more to come.

'This isn't easy for me, Jack.'

'What?'

'Trying to talk to you about . . . sex. I don't know what you know.'

'Sexing is making the piggylets, as Freya and Nodger does.'

'Sort of . . . look, what I'm getting at is . . . do you fancy her, Samantha?'

'Do not know this "fancy" word.'

'Okay then, when she was pressing herself close to you and touching your hands, what did you feel then?'

'Frights,' I tell, which is total truth. It is not a place for me to dwell. I do have understandings that this sexing is massive stuff for humanpigs. Mam and dad did make of it in earlytimes, runtygrunting as Nodger and Freya but for extra longer, and dad did make notice when the radio words got the mention of it. It is for all creatures but not me. I keep off from it because the frighteners is always at its edges, as at all those times when we is not full guarded, waiting for distraction to get full access.

Holly does the big breathing then makes her fat smile and holds the hand for splatting, which I do.

'Never mind, Jack, it doesn't matter.'

When Holly is gone and even the lemon smell of her is faded off, the bone chewing worries come back up on me and I know I must seek other intentions for my own self. One will be the looking at this Antony humanadultpig to get the scent from him. That is for the protections of Holly. She has told of his milk coloured car what sits in the path of her house.

When it is dark but before pigwallowing time, I go for the looking. I am extreme careful for the scent of human-pigboys and keep within the shadowy places. The car is milkwhite and still. I stare along the house windows and see light within Holly's bedroom and within the down rooms. With my sharpest knife I creep at one side of the car to rip the rubbery wheels. 'Hiss' is the sound I need and I do get. One time dad said you tell stuff on humanpigs by what is the way they do things not the way they say. The plan is, come back at early time, hide in the old woman shed what lives overacross from Holly. This shed is much out of any use since her man went to Jee Sus. There I plan to watch this Antony close and see what his scent is made of and I will know more of him.

Other plan is the watching for Samantha to know of any weak things of her what might be of help to me and Holly if she keeps up the coming for the irritations. But mostly of all importance is the ways to get Holly in safeness for her future life fruiting. With the knowing of dad being absolute gone from me, the dreamtimes of his return is getting blasted off. I have friended Holly, it was my approachings what made it, and in consequence I must have willingness of her total protecting. Keeping 'Freak friend' words away from her is extreme vital.

Around all this thought stuff is moon full time, with honeysuckle scents much carrying and fat growthing beneath earth. My hogear close to ground can listen on roots and tubers truffling at soil and sucking raindew for nourishing. Every place, below, this freshness, this seeking for sun energy and the giving out of full sweet air. There is a balancing within all of this as there is not up among outsideworld people. I see in them of extreme many wants what give conflictings and much dwelling on bad stuffs what lets the frighteners do their consuming thing.

TWENTY-TWO

Holly Lock's world

Mam had her 'let's not argue any more' face on when I got in. It was nearly lunchtime, no sign of Antony. When I asked if we were going to Shields, she shook her head and gave an embarrassed smile. Saturday lunchtime was usually fish and chips on the quayside at North Shields, best fish and chips in the world. No point in asking why we weren't going, it would have something to do with Antony. When I said I was having a bath she offered to wash my hair, which she hadn't done for ages, so I used the downstairs bathroom. One of Antony's shirts was hanging over the bath. She moved it without saying a word but I felt a shudder of distaste.

I guessed mam was building up to some girl talk and I decided to go along with it to try and find out what was on her mind. She used her own expensive shampoo and conditioner, instead of the supermarket own brand, which is what I usually get. That confirmed she was after something.

'This smells much better than the shampoo I've got,' I said.

'Mmmm, so it should at that price . . . there, all clean. D'you want to soak for a bit while I make some lunch?'

'I'm not very hungry.' To mam, not eating means either sickness, dieting or already full of sweets or crisps, none of which are good things in her book of rules, and it wasn't the first time I'd refused food in the last week. Sitting back on her haunches, she stared at me for so long I began to feel uneasy.

'I'm sorry we've been arguing about Antony,' she said eventually. 'But you've not been yourself either for a few days now. Is something wrong at school? Is it those bad dreams you've been having?'

How I wanted to blurt out all the stuff about Jack and Mrs Plum and Samantha. Dump it on mam, let her sort it all out. But I wasn't sure even mam would understand my friendship with Jack, let alone anyone else. They'd only see the surface, a strange man in his thirties and a teenage girl. The newspapers would go to town on it. So I knew I could never betray him, and it felt as if I'd made a sort of leap towards growing up by realising that.

Mam's eyes seemed to be burrowing into my head. I tried opening up to her a little. 'Have you ever really hated anyone, mam?'

There was quite a pause before she replied. God knows why, it was a simple enough question.

'Yes,' she said eventually, 'I hated your dad when he left us.'

'So did I. And aren't you worried that Antony might turn out the same as dad?'

'Is that why you're giving him such a hard time? Because you think he'll run off like your dad?'

'Actually, mam, I don't think I'm giving him a hard time, I'm just keeping out of his way. But yes, what's to stop him dumping us? And why does he want someone who's already got a child? Doesn't he want kids of his own?'

Mam looked as if she didn't know whether to laugh or cry. It didn't seem that complicated to me.

'It doesn't work like that, Holly. When you fall in love it just takes you over, you don't stop to see if you can tick off all the right boxes. He probably does want kids of his own, we haven't talked about that yet.'

'You mean you might think of having more kids?'

'Yes, I might. Wouldn't you like a brother or sister?'

I hadn't been expecting this so I didn't know what I thought, but the more we talked about it, the more worried I became. Not only a strange man to share the house with but possibly babies as well. Where would I be then?

'Well?' mam asked.

'I don't even like Antony, so how do I know how I'd feel about a baby?'

It was the wrong thing to say. Her face folded in on itself, and as she stood up, she gave one of her big sighs. 'I'm trying to make things better between us but all you can think about is yourself,' she said as she headed for the door. She looked back before she left and her face was as sad as I've ever seen it.

I suddenly felt lonely and vulnerable sitting in the bath. It seemed she just wanted to be with him more and more, and if I didn't go along with it, without questioning things, I was being selfish. If she found out about me wagging off school now, there'd be no sympathy.

It was as if I had no rights in the matter, no say about what happened in our lives, about who spent time in our house. She'd soon tell me if I was bringing friends here she didn't approve of.

I spent the afternoon clearing up my bedroom, pulling socks and knickers from under the bed, dusting in the dark corners behind my furniture, and thinking. If I didn't co-operate, would mam cut me right out of her life, like some inconvenience? If so, what would she do if she found out about Mrs Plum's death and disposal? How would she ever understand?

As I cleaned the leaves of my plants I noticed that one of the flowers on my fuchsia had fallen off, so I carefully pressed it between sheets of toilet paper and put it inside the pages of my wild flower book. My plan was to make a picture for the Palace with all the pressed flowers I'd saved. Jack, the pigs and the Palace were my sanctuary and despite the problems with mam and Antony I could sense, far within me, that my mind and body were starting to come together again after the horrible experience with Mrs Plum. Having convinced myself that we had no choice if Jack was to be saved, I wanted to put it in the past and concentrate on the future. Was I up to taking responsibility for Jack? Doing it secretly, without any help, dealing with Samantha's interferences and mam's fancy man? Even though I was sceptical about the tarot, I got it out. At least it gave me something to focus on.

The card was 'The Judgement'. The image shows an angel blowing a trumpet in the sky. Below, the sea is rising and naked men and women stand on small wooden boats, their arms raised to Heaven. The interpretation said:

> *It represents a point of self-reflection, at which we have to come to terms with events in our life so far, in order to avoid being consumed with regret. The card has a connection with the idea of justice and finding a balance in life. We recognise our mistakes, and if we learn from them, we can forgive ourselves and move forward. But we must be honest as we view our errors as well as our achievements.*

The tarot appeared to suggest that I was up to the task. I hoped it was right.

TWENTY-THREE

Samantha returns

After Holly's visit I get done much workings on the closing off cellar stuff. The builders over and beyond leave many things of usefulness, even made-up wall spread stuff. When it gets overpainted up on the plain paper it will be in completion and I will take Holly to seek the join where the door was. Times now I do the coming and going to within the Palace at the garden point and am extreme vigilant of outsidepeople, especial Samantha. Sometimes she lurks, as she is sniffing of the air and ground for indications, as a canine, and sometimes she arrives here extreme early and also much late. This is extra worrisome because why isn't the mam and dad searching out for her on these times? If one of my piggylets was tripping off as that, I would be full up on its trail smartly. This does mean Samantha is as a cart wheel what has lost some fixing but no body did notice and soon the cart will make a full collapse and must create devastation. It is as the song dad did sing, 'It's Just a Matter of Time', and I do feel that time creeping, as a terrible shadow, on to the Palace.

I watched for the Antony in next early times as the plan. He emerged full of the whistling and springy of feet and made a wave to an upwindow at Holly's which I taked as the mam's. He did not get the knowing of the hissed tyre till up on the road as it did hobble then. On the seeing of it he made a flapping of his hands and a head shake but not other, more angry stuff and he telled to Holly's mam to return inbed when she came to make help. He had the unhissed tyre put on extreme quick and made the whistling on all the time. He does not seem mean as the picture Holly makes and I have worries of her blocking him out when he could maybe give good comforting and supports in the outsideworld. Him and her mam together would make the strength of Nodger and Freya, true tribe leaders. And I do face to the fact that Holly, turning to me and the pigs for escaping the outsideworld, is giving up some danger to her. This does need some long thought.

The curse Samantha did put on us makes me think up on sacrifice stuff, as some how she is in that space on my inmost shelf. I have memory of dad when he telled of the boar-god what was made sacrificial at the Yule time in an other land. They put apple within the mouth for symbol of the soul-heart, as that land people had belief of apple as a resurrectioning thing. And he said that Druidpersons also speak much tales of pigs as rebirthed extreme many times. And I think extra long on this sacrifice and return to life stuff, for it may be facing up to me extreme soon.

I sleeped within the Palace properly for the first time last darkening. Freya snugged up and alongside my bed and piggylets crowded everywhere among space in between. I had a frightener dream of dad getting dead in the accident and loud hammers slumping and thrumming full through the ceiling of the Palace and big men's voices shouting out, 'Burn the Freak!' And as I did judder about within sleep, dad's voice came close at me to tell, 'Samantha will be the death of you, Jack,' which brought me crying out for dad to help and Freya fetched me to sudden wake in pushing her snout up on my face. Then, we all made tunes for some long time until sleep was weighty up on us. Still I did wake regular to stare about the darkness, hogears trembling for any slice of sound what should not be, full terrified of the outsideworld coming in to destroy me, pigs and Palace.

This next dark time is music club and Holly meets with us at the late hour previous decided to do pigwallowing. We have changed our night trekking times lots and never do go at the time Samantha knew and we did avoid any visits of her since, but my stomach depths tell me it will not be kept for long enough. I do make massive efforting to push off the frights and the whisper words dad made on Samantha, to stop them snaring up my thoughts in bitter raging. I have discovered something to show Holly this night, to lighten her. There is one owl's nest I uncovered, hard by the old beech tree what sleeps on the ground and Holly will love to witness that.

I think on dad lots now. I hold his diary books and make scrutiny at the blue words and I regard the photos of fat baby Jack in times what were good, even with the worries of mam. Before this, I pushed his recalls off away, to protect my heartpain, but always I had extra hope that he would return to me. Now I know it will not be an occurrence so I allow the thinking of him and it warms me many times. I tell all this when Holly comes and she smiles but says she never thought on her dad retrieval and I am puzzled on why.

'I don't think he loved me, not the way your dad loved you, Jack,' she tells. 'He never seemed to want to spend time with me. I don't think he ever read me a story or played a game with me or even went for a walk. And I don't ever remember him laughing, not properly, or making mam laugh. Weird, isn't it? He was my dad but he was like a stranger, even when he lived with us.'

I tell Holly of the shelf places what lives within the hoghead to hold safe all remembered things and how we might reinvite them as we desire. She thinks she has no shelves, that it is my hoghead what makes my remembrances. I tell her she will uncover those places within when it is the time. They do not spring themselves out at us straightforwardly. We have to learn of the core text and what it can do. I see when we talk of dads it makes Holly thought full and she plays her flute with more soulfilled tunes than is usual, until it is nearly time for the outsideslarking.

'Was Samantha at the music?' I ask her.

'Yeah, she was really quiet, not like her at all. She didn't make any sly remarks or try to get too close to me. D'you think hearing your mam shouting might have really frightened her, y'know, when you pretended and threw your voice?'

Within my head I think not. She will come again, *she will be the death of me . . .*

'I walked all the way to her house with her, but she still didn't want to go home, so she walked all the way back to my house. I don't know what goes on in her head. She wanted to come and stay with me but I wouldn't let her. I left her outside and went up to my room and switched the lights and music on. I peeped through the spare bedroom window about five minutes later and she was just standing there, underneath the lamppost, staring up at my window.'

'But she has gone before you came here?'

'Oh yeah, I waited for over half an hour and there was no sign of her when I came out and mam's at the pictures with Antony.'

I make explanation how I watched on the Antony last early time and did make a test on him and when I tell of my plan and consequences, her gentle eyes take up confusion. I say how I think Antony man could become something all right but Holly does not want listening on this. And still I do try further, giving thoughts to her on how she might observe him newly. Not as the one who comes up between her and the mam but as a humanpig in his own person. She still has much reluctances but I make detection of small whispers of doubt within her.

On time for the taking of pigs, I unloose the piggate extreme quiet and peek up on the everdarkening land. The outsideworld is mainly with the TV and films and the drinking up in publands and travelling tofro and shouting, and eating, but little or none do venture towards the deep darkness of Pardes Wood. None ever does in this full dark time. Behind me is Holly, Freya, Peach and all other pigs. They be together in stillness and in waiting. From a signal they come slowly outwards in pack form, full knowing that the grunting and bellowing must be hushed for the deep in places. There is pause for the locking of piggate, then advancement as one big-together-creature into the innermost wood ground. The trees this night is not bristling out to snatch, they loll and breeze about in gentleness making up fluttery musics what touches at the heartspace of things.

Up on the riverbankside, restraint goes off and plodging starts. Freya begins the dunking of some piggylets, showing to them the wallowing thing and sending me and Holly into laughing. There is scud and froth as they hive about in joyness and I get full happy as not for some long time. Holly has a face of lightness and gazes fully open to the night. I show the nest for owls and we make witness of mamtawny in nightfly and she makes glance at us as friend and it is of magic time.

'D'you think smells have colours, Jack?' Holly asks then. I am in silence for some while on that querying. 'I read about it somewhere,' she goes on. 'How blind people can smell colours. What d'you think?'

I have not dwelt on this belief in recent time so I look on inside shelves for remembrances and I find one fragment.

'I think all stuff is of one uppermost colour what can get tints to mix into every shading ever knowed of and there is the tune of the soulplace what can come together with the colours and make pure matching. So, like early years from birth time, we smell and see all colours but it gets lost as the inside head gets full with new things.'

'And do different people see colour and smells in different ways?'

I give furious nods at her quick abilities. 'In dependence of their remembrances,' I say.

'"In dependence of their remembrances",' she copies. 'That sounds like a song, Jack.' And she does make up a floaty dance for singing at these words and we give up big laughter and Freya gives some massive bellowing, so together we jump and startle to see the sudden coming up on us of Samantha.

'Thought you'd got rid of me, did you?' she says sideways. Freya trots over at her with more bellows. She will be always prepared for the fight. Holly turns tear full eyes at me and leads Freya off for the riding in avoidance of Samantha.

'My turn after you, Holly!' Samantha shouts with a sneakful voice. Peach gets to following Holly on her dancing hooves and I stay to watch the left-behinds and worry. It is more fearsome when Samantha comes closebeside. I think she is too near and I shunt away some. She moves up on me. It is in me to gather the pack together and run wild for the Palace. I do not like the unsettlingness of Samantha and her strong, too close breathing. Her scent is full of corroding and I understand she is wanting some thing of me.

'So, Jack Plum,' she says, 'I want to know what you and her get up to, really.'

I shake my hoghead slowly, inviting her to know I do not wish for the talk. She makes her eyes slit shapes and has a snorting, which is like a piglet sounds.

'Don't pretend you don't understand me. I've watched you, I've seen what you can do, I've seen you talking and laughing with Holly.'

I ask why she does the watching, why she does not have other plans to do and am given up looks of confusion.

'Holly's my friend, I want to make sure she's all right,' she says.

I think about that Holly does not much like her, but those words is full cruel and she has eyes crisp of ache. I shake my hoghead one more time and wish that she will get the boredom of my silence. Her face discovers some extra sly then and she pats her tiny hand fullover my knee.

'I think I know what you and her get up to, Jack Plum,'

Samantha says. She has the look of rabbits caught in metal trappings. 'I have secrets too, y'know,' she goes on.

I stand up extreme quick to make the hand fall off and away and I gather nearby to the water. This closetouching brings heat at all my skin. I think on the sex thing what Holly did say and wonder if this is part of that, this heated up flesh. The leftbehind pigs mill up close into my agitation. They circle of me and prevent Samantha slithering close but it does not stop the bad words she has gathered up. It does makes much agitation of me, as if the brain will crack up to the sky if she is not stilled. With gladness I see Holly retrace to us up on Freya's back. She understands something of my troubles and runs at me.

'What is it, Jack? Why are you so upset?'

Samantha gets turned in at Holly's words. I see she is fearful of Holly's anger and so will fire up her own, and there is danger they will get to splatting, so I block between them.

'It . . . it . . . it's . . . okay,' I say. My voice is got choked up. Holly glares on Samantha, who just stares full back at her, and I am knowing she wants to make hurt in Holly.

'What have you been saying?' Holly shouts.

'Leave it, Holly, it's nothing, y'know me and my big mouth.'

'What did she say, Jack, tell me?'

Samantha sighs long and turns to climb up on Freya's back without any asking. Freya looks to me and I nod for allowing Samantha the ride, to make ease on the angerful situation, but I give the permission to make stop whenever Freya wants.

'Jack, please tell me what she said,' Holly makes insistence.

I do not want the repeating of Samantha's words. I do not want Holly to know the mean thoughts. I make up words what will give some hint without too much badness.

'She says . . . as of Nodger with Freya . . . making . . . piglets . . . that it is the way of me to you . . .'

'What?' Holly's face takes up extreme shock. She is without speech now and stares over Samantha.

I tell Holly it is of Samantha's pain, it's not right on the insideout for her, some thing has gone out of her youngness. She has needs of Holly's freshness, that is why she can not be free from her. And that is the reasoning for her to make sex stuff on to Holly, to bad her up as she is.

Holly will not make a listening, she runs at Samantha as an angry sow does. 'Get off!' she yells, 'get off Freya right now!'

'I'll get off when I'm ready,' Samantha says, and as she does not understand of pig actions, so she can not make to be safe when Freya does the dump on to the mud.

'Clear off,' Holly says with much harshness, 'and this time don't come back or I'll tell your mam what you said to Jack.' Holly is full with the power of truth full words, she will not see Samantha's spoiling what does not go for truth.

Samantha makes a hurt laugh and struggles to her feet of misery. 'You don't fool me with your Miss Perfect routine. I know what you and that overgrown Freak get up to.'

'You don't know anything.' Holly's breath does come tight and short. Trees loom heavy above, branches whipping air sharply, as we disturb the rhythm of the dark wood time.

Samantha grins but it is not of joy. A shadow does come up on the moon. 'It's not right, you two being friends,' she says, and again I see within her the tangle of the outside-world, the lashing of inside pain out, on to others.

I turn at Holly and try to put some steam away but she is agitated as never before, without full awareness of the rage Samantha will spark, the men what will come with boots and dreadful spite.

'You are totally fucked up, Samantha.'

Samantha's body does tremor as a wind-buffeted flower and her voice does take on the broken sound of crackling ice.

'I'm not the one without any friends. I'm not the one who sneaks out in the dark to have sex with a fucking spastic monster.'

And then they gets to the fighting. Peach goes for protection. She bites at Samantha's leg and makes her shriek such loudness I am feared that outside people will hear and come blasting up on us. My hogears pick up a shudder below earth, as if the whole of Pardes Wood is in anger at our spoiling.

Samantha calls Peach 'bastard' and aims a kick for her small head but Freya does see and moves into it then, mauling Samantha at the ground with great hoof stamping and baring teeth. Samantha does not move, she makes a crazy whimpering what churns at me. Holly is dropped to her heels close by, she stares up on Samantha like she is something wicked.

'You're sick, Samantha. I let you come here and share my secret and all you can do is make disgusting suggestions about me and Jack. Don't you ever come near us again. Now fuck off.'

The air about us does come extreme cold, as a frost might sudden blight us, the woods, the whole world, to a deep chill. There is no taking back now, no returning from this point. Samantha will have reckoning on us.

'I hate you, Holly,' Samantha says and I hear the sobs catching up her throat and I know they will make huge shakers. I move for the comforting of her. 'Samantha . . . I . . .' I start, but she turns cruel eyes at me.

'You as well, Jack Plum. You're not a proper man.'

'We don't care what you think,' Holly says.

'This isn't finished,' Samantha shouts as she makes to hobble off. One tree lashes out to her head, catching up her hair, causing more hurt on her. She does struggle free of it and staggers into full darktime.

There comes a clumsy silence up on me and Holly in the watching of Samantha's leaving. Even the pigs is in stillness, as if they did suck up the threatening within her anger.

'This is extreme bad, Holly,' I say. 'Inside her hurt she will hurt back to us, that is the way of it.'

Holly stares up on wood darkness. The moon does clear of shadow, giving light to our misery. There is leaf rustle, the far call of ravens, and the pigs do set up low murmurings. Holly looks to the place Samantha was and I think she has the sudden wish of doing kinder words but can not tell it. 'Let's take the pigs home,' she says, extra soft, eyes and mouth both cast to earth.

We is a listless, straggly pack on the return way to the Palace. Something descends up on us, a hazy shower of a thing where there is no clearness. All of the journeying I get full alert to the distance for sounds of riot. When we become settled within the Palace Holly plays some few tunes to try for mellowing. 'Everything will be fine now that we've got rid of Samantha,' she tells as she leaves. Yet we both know, and also the pigs, that it will not.

There comes no sleep for me with all the fears so I do go within the house to make complete the over painting and for distraction of the frighteners. Within there I am in good listening for disturbance sounds which might come. The work I get done is nearby perfection, and the Palace is now sealed away off completely from the house space. I put the switch thing what makes lights go onoff within plugholes and I will do the curtains backforth every day time. If outsidepeople come to do harm I will take warning from upabove sounds and make escape at the piggate. And beyond that I have the knowing of Farmer Cotton what has the old byre with some roofing within his far fields which could make shelter of me and the pigs in dark time if that must be. There is some few bales there and space for me and all the tribe, and near by the cow troughs which carry water.

Then I do go within the boxy room to take the scent of dad into my worried places. It does wrap surround me, fetching memories of songs on star people what wait above the sky until we do find our wings. And I think of dad, out in the far dark nighttime, as one piece of star energy, watching. Later I make a search for things to give cheer and maybe show for Holly when she next comes and what I discover at the insidepocket place on dad's old jacket is a letter which might come from Eden, the place Holly would like knowledge on.

TWENTY-FOUR

Holly Lock's world

After leaving Jack and the pigs I felt like a traitor. All that stuff I'd told myself about how I could handle the responsibility and that flaming tarot reading, it was rubbish. It was my fault Samantha was trying to destroy things between me and Jack. If I'd handled her better from the start, maybe it would never have got this far. There was this horrible lump in my chest, like someone had shoved a dead cat down my throat and it was festering and throbbing. If Samantha blabbed about me being with Jack I'd get wrecked by mam. And God knows what would happen if she repeated her foul suggestion of us having sex. How could she think that? But, no matter what trouble I got into, it would all be worse for Jack. They'd find out Mrs Plum wasn't there any more and he'd never be able to deal with the police and all the questions.

I walked home very slowly and carefully, keeping close to the walls and always in the shadows. It was nearly one-thirty and the street seemed to be quieter than usual, the sound of my footsteps boomed inside my head. My mind kept doing the 'what if?' thing. What if I'd never spoken to Jack Plum? What if his mam hadn't died? That unreal haziness was with me again. I was one step removed, like an echo.

As I started to climb up the trellis back into my bedroom, Colin stepped out from the shadow of the hedge and whispered my name. It was a miracle I didn't fall and dislocate something.

'What are you doing here?'

'I didn't mean to frighten you, I came to warn you.'

The festering cat in my throat did a somersault. 'About what?'

'Your mam's been round to mine and Samantha's asking questions about you not being in school.'

More grief, that was all I needed. The energy drained out of my arms and if Colin hadn't been there to catch me I'd probably have knocked myself out. He got me to my feet just as the sound of my mam's voice penetrated the atmosphere. She was inside the house, probably outside my bedroom door, shouting my name as if the place was on fire.

Colin helped me back on to the trellis and I scrambled up towards my window. He waited till I was safely on the ledge, gave a little wave and merged back into the darkness. I had no time to wonder why he was being so helpful.

As I pulled myself into the bedroom I lost my balance again and knocked my kingfisher daisy plant on to the floor. It was like an omen, everything was destined to go wrong.

The hammering at the door started up again. 'Holly! Are you there?' Her voice was screechy, it made my heart clatter. I suddenly had visions of Samantha telling mam about me and Jack. 'If you don't answer me, Antony's going to push the door in. I mean it!' I paced the room for a few seconds, part of me terrified of opening the door and hearing what mam had to say. But there was no way out of it. I put on a pretend sleepy voice to try and bluff my way through.

'I'm trying to sleep. Leave me alone.' Furiously, I pulled clothes off and got into pyjamas as I spoke.

'We've been trying to get a response from you for ten minutes. Why didn't you answer before?' mam continued. Judging by the tone of her voice, she wasn't about to back off.

Putting my ear to the door, I could hear her and Antony whispering. 'I fell asleep with my headphones on,' I said. 'I couldn't hear you knocking.'

'Holly, why don't you just open the door so that your mam can see you're okay?' Antony said, making me bristle up.

'She wasn't bothered how I was when she went off to the cinema, was she?' There was more whispering then mam tried again, but her voice wasn't quite so manic.

'Okay, Holly,' she said. 'We don't all want to be awake all night so just open the door, let me see you're okay and we can all go to bed.'

Tousling up my hair, I moved the bed and opened the door a few inches, trying to make my eyes look bleary. They both stared at me.

'Well?'

Mam looked ready to explode. 'First,' she said, 'don't ever barricade your door again or I'll have it removed and you'll have no privacy. And secondly, Mrs Dove has put a note through the letterbox, informing me that you've been truanting.'

My throat was full of lumps, but at least she hadn't mentioned Samantha. Before I could stop her, she got hold of one of my hands, the one which wasn't holding the door, and gave a gasp.

'Your hands are freezing,' she said, then turned to Antony. 'Here, feel that,' she told him, and he bloody well did.

I pulled my hand away, closed the door and pushed the bed quickly into place. 'You might like him holding your hand but I don't want him holding mine, thank you very much,' I said. I was shocked. How could she think it was all right for him to touch me? If some stranger in the street did it she'd be horrified.

As I listened at the door I could hear Antony trying to pacify her. What about me? Who was going to give me sympathy? She tapped on the door.

'Holly, this isn't like you. Surely you can understand why I'm worried. We have to talk because I need to know what's happening.'

I held my breath until they walked away across the landing and into mam's bedroom. My stomach didn't stop folding inside out for ten minutes or more.

Their mumblings filtered through the wall for a while but things quietened down eventually and I was left with a sharp throbbing at the back of my neck, which made it hard to get to sleep. Mrs Dove had grassed me up and Samantha would do the same. I kept getting out of bed and checking the street to see if anyone was out and about. Everything was getting out of control, closing in on me. The lies, the secrets, Antony, Mrs Dove, Samantha and Colin too. What was he up to? Lying in the darkness, I weighed up my options. There was coming clean with mam about everything, asking her to protect Jack Plum. If Antony hadn't been on the scene I might have done and she might have understood. Then there was the possibility of running away, although that wouldn't help Jack and the pigs and I didn't have anywhere to hide out. That seemed to be it, not much of a choice. How much longer could I keep on lying? How long would Samantha keep her mouth shut?

These questions and loads of others orbited my skull as I took care of my kingfisher daisy. Only three of the six flowers remained intact after the fall. Did that mean I had a fifty per cent chance of surviving? It was after three when I finally dropped off. When the alarm went off at seven-thirty, I felt as if I hadn't slept at all.

TWENTY-FIVE

Things are closing in

The frighteners stay on me all the night long. I feel total ragged at the dawn time so I make the walk to Farmer Cotton's fields to look on the byre's suitableness and then walk back at extra speedy without other stoppings. I try to drive the frights off by urging my hogheart to plump extra faster. I am near full dizziness when I resume the Palace. And I get plunged then within more sad places when Holly does not visit before the schooltime. I think much on the possibles to abandon this Palace, to find some sanctuary spot where Holly would visit but Samantha does not know. But my worldview of the outsideplaces is not spacious and my hoghead provokes throbbing from the worry and I know I must give away those thoughts before the frighteners discover the accessible into me.

I feed the pigs well up and do scour out and change the hay business, then I sleep to get full strength up. My dreaming time goes in a land what is crumbling. I walk with the pigs and the ground dribbles away below us to nothing but deep wildness. All things is made up with rubber substance and we slipslide and can not make grip on one thing. The sky is absent stars and full darkness stretches to the edges of every place. I wake up with tentacles tight lashing my hogskull to make it extreme wallop. I go out and within house space to recover mam's pills. Some are for the head aches I know this, but which I may not guess so I take all back into the Palace for Holly to reveal, when she comes.

Down within the Palace I do hear the phone brrring out within the empty house. Three times it does make the ringing, until my hoghead does want to burst with the noise and fear of it. Who could know of the number? Only those what would make despair for me. Only those what would drive the Freak off from his pigs and from Holly.

It is the full aloness what is most bad. Since Holly came within the Palace I understand I had big aloness before, because of mam who did not want me, only for whisky and food and that. But Holly is become friend, she likes my words and thoughts and my pigs and has become averted to hoghead ugliness. But if she can not be coming here to us, I know the possibles of a plunge within endless frighteners and ever aloneness.

Freya rests her snout up on my lap and gives to me a pulsing time. She wants me to accept piglove and pigways. I whisper within her big sow ear all my fearings, just for letting them out of my bonce for some little while. Across her eyes and into the Palace she puts the pig knowingness and it makes a resting time for all. I give explanations that our outsidetime must be extreme late from this starting and she tells to the tribe. I will not give risk of Samantha and I have no hope of Holly for this dark time.

When I make the checks of all things to keep hogbonce busy I notice food things is too short, which is an extreme poor mistake of me, maybe brought along by all the worries of Samantha stuff. It means an outsidetrip during the light hours to the postal office of fetching mam's money and also at the shop of Mrs Robson. I shake myself up good and splash much water to wake up the face and hogskull. I plan to make the going before kiddypigs is full out and about.

This outsidetime I walk speedily as my ability. The thing is to get done extreme quick and retreat within the Palace. It is a great rush to get inout from the streets before the kiddypigs start their emergings. I move with hoghead down low but on the passing of Holly's house the Antony milkwhite car comes up on the road and I glance within the window of it. He sits and gives a back stare at me fully but I do not see the 'Freak' shape within his face, which is good, good for Holly that he is beyond that. Which gives some small lifting in my spirit.

Within the postal office there is a waiting time on account of a small outsidewoman with a titchy dog up on her arms. She buys much of stamps for places I never heard the names of. The fat man who gives service puts his droopy eye up on me all ways. He sees me within this place for extreme many years and still he makes the Freakstare. The duckyellow clock up on the wall beyond his fat head moves too quickly on and my shovel hands get damp with frightsweats so that I drop mam's money book. That small dogwoman turns for the sound and gives a shuddering at sight of my hoghead and the titchy dog makes up a pain full yap-yapping what she can not muzzle. Most all of me wants to run for some safety place but a sensible bit knows I have need of money on account of food and that makes my feet stay in solidness.

At my turn with the fat man he does his thump-stamp within the book and slithers mam's money at me without one word but does not give up the book. I wait and look and then make poor asking words.

'Tttthh . . . thhhhh . . . bbooook?' I say.

'This one is finished. Your mam will get the new one in the post,' he says. 'Do you want anything else?'

I shake the hoghead. This is not thought of, the lose of the cashing book, this was not within Holly's planning. The ache of the head comes threatening. All things seem extra fear full this light time. Mrs Robson has many outsidepeople within her shop. I move as easy as ability lets with my big shape and the plastic tub and fill up with goods. I look especial at no eyes but I know they look up on me and I hear a shivering within them and whisperings all surround me. I try to still the hogbreathing to quietness but it is extreme difficult when the frights gets so harsh and the clock spins dizzy. Mrs Robson does go 'in the back' for things and it all takes extra much worry time. When I get my things up front of Mrs Robson I hear kiddypig sounds out the distance end of the street. I want her to have some further hurry but she is much slow and olden and I can not make words that she would grasp.

Back without the noisy street I do not pause, the kiddypig scent comes extreme strong and my heart thump gets too clattering. I pick heavy legs high, put the hoghead low and make runs with rattling baggage. When I hear my name called, way back behind, filled with cross sounds, I know it is Samantha and do not turn or wait. At the finish of that street I shunt my eyes quickly back and see her and Colinpigboy on the chase of me. The heavy bags is lumbering me down and I contemplate the dumping of goods to speedy free of them. Then I hear of a voice mixed of gravel and treacle which shouts on Samantha's name. I look there to the sound and this is her dadperson. I see him only at distances many years of times but I have much curiosity of him now, for Samantha's mangling ways, and this fetches me to stop and look in deep to him. Colinpigboy stops also, as if he recognises threat in that dadvoice, and we keep space between. He is with out the pigboygang and is less of courage this day.

I notice Samantha does not want awareness to that dadvoice. I observe the falling down in her shoulders, the slumpshape of her middle and her feet as clotty cement. And way within him, the dad of her, I see much awfulness. I see it within the depth parts what he keeps hid and shaded up from outsidepeople.

But I cannot dwell on his loathingful shape, so I dash at the next line of road and Colinpigboy follows on but always with distance. I go then within the house space as I will not reveal of the garden enter to the Palace. And then I get stuck within doors because Colinpigboy flops up on the low wall to wait. Soontimes other kiddypigs come to him to make tribing and some do pitch stones on to the house outsidewalls. Their murmuring together noise sounds much as a bee battle and I have first time regretting on the sealing up I did of house and Palace. The pigs must hear on all of this stone and murmur.

One hour moves slow by and when I fear my hoghead will grow bigger, to burst with ache and worry, I hear Holly Lock's voice middling within the outside threatenings. It is of sweet and clear shape and tells them to all go 'bugger off home'. Which they do not until Mrs Lock's voice joins up to Holly's.

'Get moving, Colin Driver, and take all this lot with you or I'll phone your mam. Mrs Plum is not well and she doesn't need your bellowing outside her house. Go on!' Mrs Lock says strongly.

I am like a going-down balloon when I see they are off on their ways, my sighs come up from my feet in big billowings of betterness. Then Samantha's voice floats along the top of all other grumblings. She gets back on the street in different clothings and the dull, wasted style of face she has on her some times. It is not the slyness look, or of the foxy cunning or of the 'be my friend' glance, it is of deep snarling as a full crazy canine.

'Colin,' she calls, 'I've got something to tell you.'

I peep beyond mam's nets and I see the back of the pigboygang all tucked in. Holly and Mrs Lock are in distance and Colinpigboy and Samantha stick skulls as they move up and away. I wait for five extra minutes before I dive within the garden shading and into the sweet comfort of the Palace and welcoming pigs.

I am full with debility and bile on account of the stressing and I have no stomach for the eating so I rest my hoghead up on hay. In some time I drop swiftly within a land of no dream time, just greyish space and extreme much of it. Freya wakes me, many many hours gone, with a curious and dampened snout. The pigs is urgent for the outsidewallowing and I do make notice of some great heaviness up on my heartsoul as never before. It is as if sleeptime and dreamland have more sanctuary than everydayness. Within the Palace, folded in with the pigs, is peace, but in the outsideworld is promises of more and more fear time. Now when I do tread in the streets and woods I feel of Samantha's cursing, always lurking near as if the walls of the outsideworld is closing in at me.

The clock tells it is much late enough as I did sleep too

long, most all the day hours. I swallow up bread and a glob of cheese and jam and a mug with extra syrupy tea to encourage my muscles to heat and prepare for our outtime.

Within the silence of our packwalk to the snorting and wallowing spot I think I detect a scent of something. There is a sourness up on the air tainted with sickly sweet and I am not able to make the guess of it. I warn Freya of my tendency and she gives caution to the tribe but soon, some good time of pleasure within water and woods tells I was miss taken. I encourage Freya to release pigs from carefulness and they make much bellowing and splodging which is their need. The scent of the garlic mustard plants slinks within my hogsnout. I have memory of Holly telling that it is also named as Jack-by-the-hedge and thoughts on her pinch in to my chest. The dread is dribbling on our footsteps now, coming up on us and no escaping for both, unless I do make attentions to plan. I slump up on the favourite lying down tree and stare out at night skies to know more of the stars, in hoping that within them is meanings of all things gone and to come

The true scent of them arrives too late at my snout, and I am full surround by Colinpigboy and his pigboygang when they start up chanting, 'Pigs and Freaks . . . Pigs and Freaks!' I rise then to standing and I see Samantha lingering beyond the pigboygang but with silent urging.

'Watch me ride the pig,' she says to Colinpigboy as she turns at Freya. But I do not sanction this.

Anger rants out from me and the deeps of the sound sends the pigboygang backwards and stumbly and Colinpigboy has to make a wicked shout before they make attack at my pigs with sticks and bats. Freya and the inner pigs, the largests, turn up on them, charging, biting, arse-butting to make protection of the piggylets. Sticks and stones get hurled up and on by the pigboygang, even for the tiniest of piggylets, who squeal and shudder. And some pigboys make stone and rock thrust for me and I make allowance to the hot swamp of rage what I have pushed inmost of me. I make a shove at it out of its murky refuge and it does whack at my belly and neck and I let it come.

Colinpigboy shouts direct to me, 'You leave Holly alone, you fuckin' Freak!' His voice is breaked up as between young and grown and I do notice he is for protecting Holly, not Samantha. This gives a hesitate in my raging as it is a newfound thought but when he lifts his woody bat to do hurt of Peach I make full berserks and I pelt forwards. I grasp on the bat and lift him high up from groundspace and pitch fast round and merrygoround and I hurl far as ability. He tumblerolls and splats as he was light like twigs and it is the gasp running of other pigboys which puts the stopper into my raging. Samantha kneels next Colinpigboy and gives shakes of him but there is not any strugglings.

'You've killed him!' There is horror up on her eyes.

In bright clearness of rage I tell she should not have brought him to my pig place.

She knows I speak truth and she sobs and all pigboys do run as frighted hens. I struggle at my choky throat and make words, as it is extreme necessary to give Samantha trueness. First I make the pulse thing Holly showed and I find Colinpigboy is not with death.

'Sss . . . aman . . . tha,' I say, 'Colinpigboy makes breathe.' And she punctures some little bit. 'Samantha, lll . . . list . . . listen at me. It . . . it is wrong . . . th . . . the hurt your ddd . . . dad does at yyyy . . . you. I do . . . see it.' But before I finish she is gone running. She runs but she will not ever make free of the knowing what I saw and spoke of. And my hope is that she will take it inmost, that it is not she with blame, as it was not me to blame for mam's miserypain.

I lift Colinpigboy up on shoulders as a scarf might be, he is much light as a bag of boiled bones. And I gather up the anxious stomping and much hurt tribe. They have bad cuts and there is much bruising to come through and Freya has the hobble on her gait. Within the Palace I wash and pat anti septic up on sores and cuttings and make washings with fresh water to give coolness, then I fodder and give full new hay, and I sing soft of better times and secret places in times to come along.

Colinpigpoy I put to lie up on one bale with chequered blankets overlaying him. I hear the gasping sound of when he is awakened. I see he is full with worry of being within the Palace and shrinks up on himself with no word to spit.

I feel a want to hurt him more, for revenge of the tribe, and I press it back and away. But he does see the want in me, I know it fully. When I get sure the pigs is in rest I carry Colinpigboy to outside, up around my neck but with his eyes covered in tight ribboning. He must not know of the true Palace situation so I go down far into the wood edges and ramble some before I let his eyes free. He shivers some as we move slow and quiet for sight of his house and there in the dark time, in low glow of lamppostlights, his pigboygang and Samantha wait at silence. His grizzly mam stands foldedarms next the gate, also in waiting. Colinpigboy wriggles and sobs up on my neck as he has sense of approaching his home and I understand crisis time and I find slow words come to my mouth to whisper warnings on him.

'Do not . . . come . . . near by mm . . . me or . . . my pigs aa . . . again . . . Colinpigboy,' I say. 'Not . . . yyy . . . oo . . . or yy . . . yyyour pigboygang.'

He becomes as limp things, as wet towels, after these issued words, and I lower him, not carelessly, to the ground near by to his mam. She looks to my eyes that she must shout and ratchet but in surprise, she gathers something in from me what stops a rant. She puts tenderest arms up on her pigboy to lead him to within. Colinpigboy looks once back to me beyond the arm of his mam and I know he has heard truly of my intention and will give respect at it. Whether out of frights, or of knowingness, it will be.

Samantha runs off away when I turn backwards. Even within the shape of her sobbing I do see she is bent full for troubles. I was miss taken to give an acknowledge at the true shape of her pains. I sense now that she might fetch pure treachery to us. At Holly Lock's gate the Antony stands. He did be observer of proceedings and his face is not feared or in hostile, it is bright with questions but the exact type I do not decipher and there is no word to be shaped between us, but neither is there the loathing or frights. There is no light within Holly's room and I make hope that she is deep asleep and beyond the knowing of this event. And I make wishes of Samantha not to do shameful stuff on Holly. But my knowledge on her and the pain she carries tells that there is no way of escape from it, for me. From that first longing moment of knowing Holly, through the past times of watching and waiting and making gifts at pigrelicstone and wishes up on the Boar star, some far within part of me did know it would arrive to this place. Letting the outsideworld in to my Palace with Holly did give possibles access to all its despairs.

TWENTY-SIX

Holly Lock's world

Things have gone downhill at school. When I arrived for afternoon register Mrs Dove had me in her room for a 'chat' about how disappointed she was at me nicking off school. I didn't deny it, there was no point. She wanted to know if something was wrong, if she could help in any way. If only. Neither Samantha or Colin were in school, so at least I didn't have them to deal with. When I got home there was a note from mam waiting for me, saying she wanted to talk to me properly about wagging off school. Fortunately she was out with you-know-who-so I made sure I was tucked up when they got back. When she looked in on me, I pretended I was asleep. She wasn't going to let the truancy go, though, I knew that, so I had to come up with something convincing. It was miserable, though, not seeing Jack and Peach and the other pigs for a whole day and night, like I'd lost something that made me feel special.

At one-thirty in the morning I came wide awake with horrible pains in my back and stomach. Feeling like death warmed up, I got out of bed to search for painkillers and nearly passed out when I saw the bloodstains on my lovely lilac sheets, just like a great red scar. We've done menstruation to death at school so I knew what it was, of course, and mam must have been through it half a dozen times as well, it's just that I wasn't expecting it to start in the middle of the night.

I stripped off my pyjama bottoms and the bed sheets and put them to soak in my sink. The stain had gone right through to the mattress so I cleaned it up with my facecloth and some shampoo, it took ages. Making a pad with loads of folded toilet paper inside some old knickers, I put clean jama bottoms on under my dressing gown. I knew where the tampons were but I wasn't ready to chance them, they looked too painful. Mam got pains with her periods so I was used to her knocking back the painkillers every month and sometimes sitting with a hot water bottle.

The ache was like having a heavy weight tied to the bottom of my stomach, dragging me down towards the floor and making me feel really sorry for myself. But a bigger part of me was also pleased that it had finally started.

The label on the pill bottle said 'one or two tablets every four hours', so I took two, anything to stop the agony. I filled the hot water bottle and made a drink of hot chocolate and I'd almost got back to my room when Antony appeared on the landing.

'You all right?' he asked when he saw me.

There was no way I was going to tell him. 'Fine,' I said, walking past him as quickly as my dragging weight allowed.

'Did the kerfuffle in the street disturb you?' he asked the side of my head.

'What?' I said irritably.

'That lad Colin and the big backward fellow from down the end, Jack something.'

I suddenly became fully alert. I stopped walking but tried not to look too interested. 'What happened?' I asked.

Antony indicated for me to follow him downstairs so we didn't wake mam. He took the mug of hot chocolate and carried it for me and nodded at the hot water bottle. 'What's that for?' he asked.

'To stop me being abducted by aliens,' I said, and I was startled when he broke into a quiet laugh.

'You really are hard work, Holly, y'know that, don't you?' he said.

'I thought you were going to tell me about Colin.'

He nodded and switched the kettle on. 'First things first,' he said. 'I've got a belting toothache, where does your mam keep the painkillers?'

My mind was on overdrive as I watched him swallow three pills. When he eventually sat down at the kitchen table with a mug of tea, I'd convinced myself that Jack must be in prison and the pigs all alone and miserable. I was relieved when I got the story out of him, but then immediately tense as I realised Samantha was responsible. When I caught the end of Antony calling Jack backward again, I reacted angrily.

'He is not backward,' I said. 'Don't call him that.'

'Okay, okay, what shall I call him then?'

'Just bloody well call him by his name, Jack Plum.'

Antony shook his head and pressed his lips together. 'Can't you give me a break, Holly? I'm not really the enemy, and my bloody tooth is killing me.'

I wanted to tell him that his pain was probably not half as bad as mine, but I didn't, of course. My mind was too full of Jack and what Colin's mam might be up to and whether Samantha was planning more trouble. The hot water bottle resting on my stomach gave me some respite and when Antony suggested toast and peanut butter I agreed. He didn't try and drag me into any more conversation and when I decided to take my toast upstairs he just gave a little wave.

The mattress was definitely too wet to sleep on so I made a bed on the floor with a spare duvet and curled up around the hot water bottle. The pains receded and my eyelids got heavier by the second. I made a plan to go and see Jack before school and as I fell asleep I realised that my feelings towards Antony were softening a little. Not that I was going to admit that to mam, or him. Not yet anyway. As I finally dropped off I clung to the hope that Samantha was going to keep her mouth shut about me and Jack.

TWENTY-SEVEN

Palace time is running out

The Palace is packed up with restless flutterings all the dark time long. Freya and the other growing sows do their best with licks and comforts for the piggylets and their hurts. I feel great lumps of sadness on my insidethroat when Freya looks to me. I am the supposed guardian of all them, pig protector, and I failed. Conflict thoughts have raddled at the hoghead the dark through and I have full understandings that the fetching of Holly within the Palace made this outsideworld risk extra close. That the lack of pigsense from out there leaked in up on us, dripping meaness and cold misery. It was my needings for humanpigkind, my aloneness what has gathered pain in and on the pigs and I feel full shamed.

One considered thing is to send Holly back away from us, not just for pig protection but for her safeness. The volcano in the outsidethere always seethes to be rid of the Freaks. If she has attachment to Freaks she will be full at the mercy of eruptions, as us insidepeople. And way far back inmost the hoghead a crumbling voice, something shaped as dad's, whispers at me, '*It is too late.*' I listen in with that voice in the all-night hours and I hatch plans, new plans and undertakings.

Outsidepeople cannot be changed hurriedly. In the glimmery moon light I take acceptance of that and it comes up on me that Holly must be untethered of the Freak, me. It is as past times sacrificials, soul heart stuff, what means I can gift her full life futures. It is in my choosing to make this hoggifting.

Holly makes extra danger at coming within the Palace too long before the schooltime. She gets full with horror at the hurts of all the pigs and she cries saltiness up on Peach at her cuddling. Then she does take the shaming of it to her own self.

'It's all my fault, Jack, not being able to handle Samantha properly. I'm so sorry.'

'Many differing faults,' I say, 'not one only. If you had not come within to us, then at the death of mam what would we have got to?'

That gives her a brightening bit and when she begins the cursing and threats at Samantha I give her knowledge of the true state, the Samantha dad, the deep cruel stuff, and Holly's mouth goes as a tunnel of disbelieving and more horror takes up her face.

'You can't be sure of that, Jack, you're just guessing,' she says.

'It is truth,' I tell.

This brings up the sighing thing and some pacings.

'She wanted to tell me a secret but I wouldn't listen.'

'Not your fault, Holly.'

'Anyway, even if it is true, it's no excuse. If she'd left me alone, kept her fucking nose out of my business . . . and Colin, why does he always do what she wants?'

She is bringing her thinking upout loud to me and I can tell confused stuff has her.

'Colin made this attack on account of you, Holly. He telled it to me, "Leave Holly alone, you Freak!" Colin and Samantha both have carings for you.'

'No, they don't. They hurt you and they hurt the pigs and that bitch is threatening me. Why don't you want to punch them, hurt them back for what they've done? I do. If I was as strong as you I'd –'

She looks to me filled of perplexions. It is of difficulty, the holding back of hate, especial for young girlpigs. It is a learning thing what takes full time to grow.

I give explaining on how humanpigs can make badness but not be total unfit soul hearts. And, learnings can come up to them but not on account of more wrongness. In my seeing, Samantha and Colin can take these learnings, and I tell Holly she is the one for showing.

'So you think it's all my fault, Jack? If I'd been kinder to Samantha and more sympathetic to Colin, maybe things wouldn't have gone so wrong. Is that what you're saying?'

'No, Holly, it is not of that. I made the connect to you on my desires of humanpig linkings to me. I did make this all come thundering. I have miscarried you and failed on my pig duty. It is me for blaming.'

Changes is coming within her face, maybe of Samantha's true pains and of Colin's losing, and I have the guess that Holly may make the break of Samantha's silence. Samantha has all times seeked her out and for maybe this purpose. And she may give the friend hand to Colin. Maybe, it is all of that but in possibility. All of this I tell to Holly. She will not presume of my new plan but it is behind all this telling, the warning in the dad-voice-within told me realtrue. Palace time is being run away.

I tell her of the phone what keeps brrringing within the house, time on time on time. She thinks on it and tells it may be the people what sent the especial letter on the insurance stuff.

'Just ignore it, Jack, you never answer the phone anyway.'

'It did never hardly brrring past times. The sound does raddle me, Holly, it winds up like clamps up on my head.'

'Then we'll just unplug it and it won't ring at all. Okay?'

This she does for me and just at the time of her leaving, with her face burdening what she now knows, I remember my finding the letter within dad's jacket. It is a message and I give it into Holly's hands for reading.

'Is it from Eden?' I ask. She looks and shakes at her head in some puzzlement.

'No, it's not. I'll read it to you . . . "Dear Dan, I know you're unhappy and I wish I could be with you more often. I think your idea of taking Jack somewhere new, away from all the blame and violence and accusations, is the right thing to do. You know I'd come with you if I could . . ."' Holly stops the reading and stares to me but I do nod for the continuing. '". . . but my parents would come looking for me and get the police involved and that wouldn't help you at all. You could keep in touch, though, let me know where you both are. Take this chance, Dan. Love Babs."'

Holly reads at the whole of it again, then she makes the big sigh thing and her eye brows do pucker up.

'I can't believe it,' Holly says with big breaths between, like she has sobs waiting. 'It's from my mam, I recognise her writing. When I asked her about you, all I got was the "Stay away from Jack Plum" stuff. But she was friends with your dad, real friends at one time, don't you think? How come she didn't say something?'

'Past and gone stuff, Holly,' I say, because it is my realisation of things with the outsidepeople. 'Things is put in pretend boxes, like past things and maybe things and regret things, and they is not to be talked about in the now, unless it is forced to be so.'

Holly stands up full and her body does the sagging thing as she is full of new weights. I regret the telling of Samantha's misery now as it is piled up with news of Babs the mam and secrets. Too much for one small humanpig in one day time but the inside voice keeps its urging up on me: *Palace time is running out.'* The pigs is in full quiet, licking and making rest and I show to Holly mam's pill packets and ask for the word meanings for pig comfortings. That does stir her.

'I don't know if they'll work on pigs, Jack,' she says.

'Humanpig and pigflesh extreme close in,' I say and she makes her nods.

'Okay, Jack,' she says with a laying out of the packs and bottles. 'These are ordinary painkillers, paracetamol, but they can be dangerous if you take too many all at once, no more than two at a time for adults, so probably one for big pigs and half for little ones. And these,' she points at the silvery strips of midget ones, 'these are called morphine and they're really strong. My Uncle Jimmy took it after he got his new hip in and he said he felt like he was flying, so I wouldn't use them at all, Jack.'

I tell her to go for schooltime and say not one thing to Colinpigboy and pigboygang, not of the bashing of pigs, as it will make her seen as 'with' Freaks. And those who is 'with' Freaks does get treated same as. I get her to make the promise, the promise of silence.

'That's not fair, Jack, why should they get away with it? And why should mam get away with lying to me?'

I make explanation how not one 'gets away' because there is suffering for all in differing ways what may be not seen by others. She takes up a stillness and drops within her own thoughts. But she gives the sparky smile when I ask if she will return to the Palace soon beyond schooltime and she does make promise of it.

She holds her titch hand at mine for the splat deal and I linger at the warming of her touch. Holly leaves us with more cuddling comforts for the pigs. I have much preparations to make.

TWENTY-EIGHT

Samantha's revenge

My kingfisher daisy looked a bit miserable when I left for school. Me and it both. I was in a sort of bubble all morning, feeling cut off from everybody and full of anger. If Jack was right and there was a good reason why Samantha was such a total bitch, I didn't care, I still wanted to push her face out of the back of her head. Fortunately she wasn't in school for registration and someone said she was sick, but when I realised Colin Driver wasn't in school again either, I began to panic.

During the first two lessons, which were English with Mrs Dove, all the stuff about mam and Jack's dad kept chasing round my head like some internal demon so I couldn't concentrate at all. How could she have cared about his dad and then treated Jack as if he was a freak? It didn't make any sense to me. What was she frightened of? I was shocked by her secrets and lies and couldn't understand her behaviour in not really considering my feelings over Antony. Maybe she would say the same about me deceiving her, but I was protecting Jack, and who was she protecting except herself? There was no way I could pretend I didn't know about it because I was sure it would show on my face the very next time I saw her. Whichever way I looked at it, I knew it had to come out.

Mrs Dove kept me behind at the end of the lesson and wanted to know if I was all right – again. When lunch break came and there was still no sign of Samantha or Colin, that dead cat climbed back inside my throat and I legged it for home.

I wanted to call on Jack first but when I got to the end of the street I could see two men at his front door and they didn't look like salesmen or the Bible brigade. I watched from behind a hedge and saw them knock and try to open the front and back doors of the house and then wander around the garden before returning to their car. But they didn't drive off, they just sat there waiting. Then I realised they might be from the insurance company and a ripple of heat up my spine told me this was not good news. I desperately wanted to warn Jack about them but I couldn't risk being seen when I wasn't sure who they were, and anyway, I guessed he'd be down in the Palace and he was always very cautious when he came out of there.

Back home something was wrong. I knew it as soon as I opened the door. The place should have been empty, with mam at work and Antony gone to wherever he goes, but it wasn't, they were both there and they looked like trouble.

'Holly, oh my God!' Mam said. 'Where have you been? We've been phoning the school and they've been looking all over for you. We were so worried. Where have you been?'

'I had a headache, I just wanted to come home for a rest,' I lied. Antony's eyes felt like they were turning me inside out.

'You should have told someone you were coming home.'

'All right, all right, what's the panic all of a sudden?'

Antony put his hand on mam's arm. 'I think we should all sit down, don't you?' he said.

Mam nodded and made to put her arm around me but I pulled away. I felt as if there was suddenly no air in the room, like I could hardly breathe, and I was frightened. Why were they both here? What was going on?

'Why aren't you at work?' I asked.

'Antony's right, Holly, we should sit down, then we can talk.'

'What about? About why I nipped home from school in my lunch break? What's all the fuss about, I've done it before.' Things were not looking good.

'No, Holly, not that. Come on, sit down,' mam said. There was something in her voice that knocked me sideways and I let her lead me to the sofa. 'I don't want you to be frightened, we're not angry, we're just concerned and we need you to be truthful with us.'

I didn't like the royal 'we' at all, it was like she'd suddenly become half a person.

'I'd rather talk to you on my own,' I said, and to my surprise Antony just nodded at mam and went off into the kitchen. That's when I knew I was in deep trouble.

'This is not a game, Holly, it's very important, right? Now I know all kids keep things from their parents, for all sorts of reasons and most of the time that's all right –' she said before I interrupted her.

'And parents keep things from kids as well,' I said pointedly. I knew Samantha must have said something about me and Jack.

'Yes, they do, but often that's for good reasons.'

'I have reasons.'

'Look, Holly, I don't want this to turn into an argument. There are some things which shouldn't be kept secret and sometimes things can get out of hand and . . .'

She was beginning to struggle for words and I had the urge to say, 'Just get to the point' – but what I wanted most of all was to be on my own so I could go and see Jack and warn him about the two men.

'I want to go to my room,' I said. 'I'm tired, I want to lie down. Can't we talk later?'

'No, Holly, we have to do it now. I know it's all connected with why you haven't been in school –'

'What is?'

'Look . . . I've . . . I've told you not to go into Pardes Wood without me or another adult, haven't I?'

'I don't go without an . . . an adult.'

'Samantha says you do, she says she's seen you there.'

'She's a liar. Ask anybody at school, she's always at it.'

'Holly, she says she's seen you there with Jack Plum, she says you go and visit with him all the time.'

'She's trying to cause trouble as usual. She exaggerates everything, she's a bitch and I fucking hate her.'

'Holly, stop it, just calm down and listen.' She held up my flute book. It was open at the page where I'd practised Mrs Plum's signature.

'What's this all about?' she asked. I didn't respond, I couldn't think of a convincing lie.

'Samantha said –' mam went on but I cut her off.

'She's a liar, I've told you.' I was thinking of spilling the beans about Samantha and her dad but I realised I only had Jack's say so on that. Part of me was hoping I still might bluff my way through, but I hadn't bargained for the rest of what mam had to say.

'Samantha is very upset, Holly. She says Jack Plum takes his clothes off –'

'No, that's not true. She's the one who wanted him to . . .' I stopped because I knew I'd blown it and I knew I had to get out of the house. If Samantha was saying stuff like that about Jack all hell was going to break loose. The walls of the room appeared to be closing in on me. The sound of Antony making tea in the kitchen was coming at my ears from the end of a long tunnel.

'You were there, then,' mam said. 'Why did you lie about

it?' I didn't reply. 'He hurt Colin Driver very badly, Holly, and I want to know –'

There was no point in lying any more. The shit had already hit the fan. Sweat crawled down my back and my lips began to tremble as I shouted, 'Colin Driver deserved to be hurt, in fact I'd like to bang his head on the wall till it bleeds. If you'd seen what him and his gang did –'

'Holly, you're not making sense. Samantha's hurt, the doctor says . . . well, he says . . . she's got bruises all over her back and legs and . . . she's . . . she's been . . . sexually assaulted.'

Mam's words boomed around the room: *sexually assaulted*. Oh Christ, Jack was right then.

'She fell off Freya's back, that's how she got the bruises –'

'Freya? Who's Freya? Holly, please tell me, has Jack Plum hurt you too, like he has Samantha?'

'Jack didn't hurt Samantha. He would never ever do that. I told you, she's lying . . . she's fucking lying . . . Maybe she has been sexually assaulted, but not by Jack . . .' Suddenly I became clammy all over, getting in a major panic about Jack and what those men might be doing. When I tried to stand up my legs felt like sponge. Mam rushed over and put her arms around me.

'Holly, I need to know you're all right.'

I pulled away from her.

'I'm perfectly all right. But you're not listening to me. What's the point of talking to you? Jack hasn't hurt me or

Samantha, he wouldn't – and talking of secrets, why didn't you tell me about you and Jack's dad?'

I waited as her face suddenly flushed up. She didn't know how to react. There she was, telling me off for being secretive and here I was catching her out at the same thing. It was as if I could read her thoughts on her face. She was wondering if it would all have turned out differently if she'd been honest with me when I first asked about Jack Plum. And maybe it would have been.

Her voice was quiet and hesitant when she finally spoke. She admitted she'd been friends with Mr Plum and I could tell it had been important to her. And of course he'd died, at the height of that friendship. I wanted to throw my arms around her and tell her how it could all be sorted out, that Jack could be saved if she supported him. But before I could move or speak she destroyed the moment by continuing to see him as the problem.

'That was a long time ago, Holly. Who knows what Jack's capable of now?'

I stood up to interrupt her this time. 'Jack Plum is kind and gentle and clever and you made me think he was a Freak.' I moved to the hall door. 'I don't want to talk to you any more, I'm going to lie down.' Once I was through the door I bolted for my room and barricaded myself in and checked the back lane before climbing out of my window. Praying that Jack would be okay, and so focused on getting to him, I didn't see Colin, lurking in a gateway, until he stepped out in front of me.

'Where you going?' he asked.

'None of your business. Get out of my way.'

'If you're looking for the Freak, he's gone. We broke in, the place is empty.'

'You're disgusting, d'you know that? You've got no right to call him a Freak and no right to break into his house.'

'After what he did to you and Samantha –'

'That's all lies.'

'She says –'

'I don't give a fuck what she says. I was there, Jack never laid a finger on her or me. But you can tell her that I'm really gonna hurt her, when I see her, for all the trouble she's caused.'

I pushed Colin out of my way. He didn't resist. His whole body had slumped, as if my words had really got through to him. I felt a rush of sympathy but I didn't have time to do anything about it. I walked away slowly and at the corner of Jack's garden turned to make sure Colin couldn't see me. The men and the car had gone from outside the house. One less problem to worry about. I crept into the garden, checking carefully all the time in case anyone was watching me. And as I approached the entrance to the Palace something very cold seemed to cling to me for a moment.

TWENTY-NINE

Time to go

When Holly does come finally, I is half lying up on the hay. All the pigs is close by and in full stillness. She makes immediate notice of changes within me and takes fear up on her.

I tell her how some men came, hammer hammer on the updoors with big shouts, wanting mam. And I say how I did know of their coming early times, how I did guess on it. Then pigboys came also to lash brick stones on the upwindows, stamp about upsteps, and call at the Freak to show. I make explanation it is the ending of the Palace, that time is run off complete.

'No, Jack, listen, we can tell them the truth. Mam knows I've been with you now and that I know about her and your dad and she'll have to listen to me and make them listen. We can stop all this, you can live with the pigs –'

I tell how she must not put the fight up as I have knowledge of the ending. They wants me for the damage of Samantha, that was in the pigboy shouts. The damaging is much real as I telled before times and the Freak must have the blaming of it. It is the outsideworld way. They know Freaks by the shape of their face and body and ability with words and such, that is what they believe. The kiddypigs is only listened at if the pictures is agreeing with the adultpig views. I say how decisions is made up all ready and the big stones what will crush the Palace is rolling fast at us. And I say then how I did plan on this departing much before and it is the proper undertaking and that I have one difficult thing to ask from her. I make fast words, fear full that my senses will depart me and Holly is much troubled at this.

'Jack, please, don't let them drive you away. Please, I couldn't stand it, you're my friend, my best friend.'

Salt water flows off her eyes and her small body lunges with sobs and anger. I tell her the full truth of my plan, of swallowing the morphine, and that the pigs are in knowing of coming events. That in soonest time we must make the tracks at the old byre of Farmer Cotton's, all pigs, me and her. And all along the way I will swallow up the full lot of paracetamols and morphines. Holly's eyes gets swimming of tears and her mouth makes big tremors.

'No, Jack, no, you can't do that. Let me get the doctor, please!'

'This I want, Holly, it is my true wishing. I do not want to be attached to the outsideworld, there is no trusting in it for me, no good futuretime. You is my best friend and I ask you to take my wish up. I did make thoughts on hogman resurrection stuff, as the seven magic pigs what is in the story on the King of Golden Pillars. These pigs' bones was laid in full energy sun one day from death time and come the cusp of day to nighttime, their souls did come into new pigs to get another birthing. But time is extreme shortening on us and can not fulfil that. There is no place back from this, Holly, not for me and not for you, believe it, please, before we is too late for escape.'

She shudders some more big sobs and wipes of the snot and tears up on her sleeve and hugs close into me. I feel the quavering within her, the hotness up on her head. Freya does snort deep. It is warning, danger will be coming.

'Freya is telling, Holly, time does run off.'

She pulls softly from me and I gather her consent to take acceptance of my plans within her eye message, and I do understand how that means she is in more learning of the nature of outsideworld people than before times.

'When I is full dead, Holly, you will tell Freya the time is come for the eating of that body what is then without soul and I will be for ever in and within the pigs. That is the way me and pigs shall not get parted off. It is only one way it can be. You must be total freed of the Freak connection. Will you do of that thing?' I go to silence then for her to have thought time. When she remains unspeaking I have fear I ask too big things of her.

'Is this watching of my dying an too awful request, Holly?'

She shakes her head very slow and presses her two lips hard as to prevent more sobs.

'I don't want to lose you, Jack,' she tells.

'I am in knowing of that, Holly, and I is filled up of gloom in the losing of you, but I did dwell up on this longtimes and it is the full right way. Will you still be with us, and make the watching, for me and for the pigs? And after, take us to the pig fields to mix and moulder in with Farmer Cotton's tribe, where Nodger will make ease of the coming?'

She nods slow. She is too trembly to make up words. And up above we hear of more smash noise and more stomp and shout so we hoard to the piggate in the silent fright way. I am wobbly on the feet but I take a wood plank for a stick to balance and we struggle off, all in close together as a tribe should be. We reach to the edges of Pardes Wood with no incidence. The trees lean in at me and give tender touches as if in knowing what is becoming and Holly makes more sobs and the pigs give beast snortings in their rage at humanpig kind. Freya and tribe know that their younglings is ate by them and that their flesh is made use in other ways. It is within pigmemory and is passed on all ways. And I think maybe I really is half hog as I see pigworld as a homeplace and pigsense as my own. And I do have belief that the possession of a tail for the telling of inside emotionals is much more of truth than the smile of humanpigs what can be pretend and false. The tail move is never pretend, it is deep down instinct reactions to within feelings.

I am in full weakness at coming into the byre and drop to the ground with easiness. Holly makes gasps and sighs as she will bring on massive hurting sobs to herself, but I point for the sky which is moon full and brimming of stars what do spangle.

'Are you really sure about this, Jack?' Holly says. 'I can get to a phone quickly at Farmer Cotton's and have an ambulance here in no time. And we can show all those bastards who want to hurt you what a kind and clever person you really are. Why should you die, Jack? Why should I lose you? They're the bad ones.'

'Time for acceptances,' I tell. 'It is soon the time for me to go within my pigs. And you, you must become something, Holly, for me. You must grasp at the world, go out into it, give it your brightness and cleverness and your ability to give love. Make huge plannings, Holly, make massive adventurings. My soul thing will be around all ways, filled up with proudness of what you will become in that outsideworld. Do it for me and for pigs everywhere. And Holly, do not be extreme harsh at Samantha, she is filled of pain and she will need you to give her wisdom on all of this.'

Holly does look away and I asks again and get one small nod.

My life starts to be sucked from out of me like a worn-out balloon and I must drop all limbs into dark nothingness. Even my words is losing the breath.

'Goodbye . . . brother and sister pigs . . . goodbye, Holly . . . I love you . . . all.'

I sat there for a long, long time, just staring at Jack's lifeless body, hoping that I really was in a bad dream and would soon wake up. The moon had disappeared behind cloud and I began to feel the cold. But when Freya nudged me with her snout, I knew what was expected of me. Jack looked so full of peace lying there with the pigs all over him snuffling and snorting and hissing. I'd promised to protect him, to stop him being taken away and locked up and I'd failed. He'd known better than me how difficult it would've been to get the truth out into the open. And I knew that in giving up his own life he was protecting me.

I waited until there had been no pulse or breath for ages, until his skin was cold as ice-cream, and then I removed his clothes. The pigs stood around us in a circle, giving me space but urging me on. In the far, far distance I could hear police sirens.

I moved away to let the pigs do their part. Freya nudged me away even further. I turned my back on them and spoke out loud, hoping the departing soul of Jack Plum would hear me and also to block out the sound of cracking bone and ripping flesh. The hyacinth moon slipped out from behind the clouds, come to say farewell too.

'Goodbye, Jack Plum, I'll miss you and I'll always be glad you made me your friend.'

Lying on the damp grass, staring up at the sky, the thought came into my head that there was something weird and wonderful about the whole thing. I can't explain it, but it was sort of like those words they say in church: *'Eat of my body, drink of my blood and you shall have everlasting life.'* And in that moment, I realised that Jack was right about not dwelling on stuff like hate and revenge. How if you did, it would eat away at your own life and I understood he knew so much more than I ever realised.

Freya and her pigs surrounded me. In the light of the moon I could see their snouts were stained with blood, their bodies smeared with gore. There was nothing much but oily stains and some bone and gristle left of Jack, dark ruby stains on the floor of Farmer Cotton's byre. As I looked around I saw lights flashing over the fields, a helicopter hovered in the distance and voices called out my name. It was time to go.

I gathered the pigs around me, ran towards Farmer Cotton's fields and said my farewells to them. Then I stared up at the star-sparkled sky and whispered my final goodbye to Jack.

I left that body much before Holly gave my pigs the signal for chomping. I soared up at the byre roof, saw into her braveness, watched Freya and the tribe at their consumptions, fetching that body what was mine into them for ever time.

What is done is for best. Holly now is free to grow into rich fullness. And I know that I am now just soul, full energy soul, as dad did make prediction. And best of it all, I hear his dadvoice close at me, telling words of great loving and pleasure that I am to come beside him for all times future.

Acknowledgements

Huge thanks to the following who provided support and encouragement during the writing of this novel, especially during periods of self-doubt: Peter Mortimer, Jo Williams, Chrissie Glazebrook, Sally Walker, Deborah Carey, Niaull Culverwell, Val McDermid Liz White, Lorna Powell, Katrina Coleman and members of Cloud Nine Theatre Productions.

For invaluable research support: Emily Edge, Lucy Mounter, Jack Williams.

For professional support; Wendy Logan and Tracey Russell.

For publishing my earlier fiction: Brandon, Iron Press, The Leveller, Sheba and Women's Press.

I was supported during the writing of *Pigtopia* by a Northern Writers' Award from New Writing North and have now received a Hawthornden Fellowship to work on my next novel *The Sound of Skin.*

Last but certainly not least, many thanks to my brilliant agent Patrick Walsh for his tireless enthusiasm; to my talented editor Angus Cargill; to Bill Clegg; to Jon Riley and all at Faber & Faber and to everyone at Conville & Walsh for all their hard work.